"What good is your life going to be to you if you're dead?"

"About the same as it is if I'm not in control of it."

Clarke's stare was not kind. Or gentle. It was pointed. Searing. She didn't flinch. Or back away. In fact, her chin lifted a bit as she glared back at him.

"Are you telling me that you were wrong? That you don't think the killer will be there tonight?" Everleigh asked. "Or that you don't feel you have a good chance, the quickest chance, of finding out what's going on, if you're there?"

"No. But I might have misjudged the danger to you in going to the party," he said.

"And I might have misjudged the danger to you in hiring you," she shot back. "I'm like a time bomb and you're right beside me. If I explode, you could die, too. Or be badly hurt." It wasn't like he'd be any more capable of stopping a flying bullet aimed at them than she would.

* * *

The Coltons of Grave Gulch: Falling in love is the most dangerous thing of all...

* * *

If you're on Twitter, tell us what you think of Harlequin Romantic Suspense! #harlequinromsuspense

Dear Reader,

Welcome to Grave Gulch! I'm bringing you a unique and special story, one that took me places I'd never been before. At the start of the book, our heroine, Everleigh, is just getting out of prison, having been put there accused of a murder she didn't commit.

I've never been in a prison or jail for more than a few minutes of observation. But I know how it feels to have to pay for something that I didn't do. I know how it feels to be trapped. I know how hard it is to hold on to hope during those times. And Everleigh came along and rescued me. She showed me how to feel all the hard stuff and still hold on to hope. She gets up every morning and gives what she has to the day ahead—even when it means working with the man whose family put her away.

In addition to Everleigh, we've got all kinds of other good stuff here in Grave Gulch. Suspense. Murder. A possible serial killer in the background. Gossip. Drama. A deranged forensic scientist. A big family of independent thinkers who risk their lives for the good of their community. And, of course, love.

So come on in. Sit with me for a while and I'll do my best to make you glad you did.

Tara Taylor Quinn

COLTON'S KILLER PURSUIT

Tara Taylor Quinn

Special thanks and acknowledgment are given to Tara Taylor Quinn for her contribution to The Coltons of Grave Gulch miniseries.

Recycling programs for this product may not exist in your area.

ISBN-13: 978-1-335-62882-4

Colton's Killer Pursuit

This edition published by arrangement with Harlequin Books S.A.

For questions and comments about the quality of this book, please contact us at CustomerService@Harlequin.com.

Harlequin Enterprises ULC
22 Adelaide St. West, 40th Floor
Toronto, Ontario M5H 4E3, Canada
www.Harlequin.com

Printed in U.S.A.

Having written over ninety novels, **Tara Taylor Quinn** is a *USA TODAY* bestselling author with more than seven million copies sold. She is known for delivering intense, emotional fiction. Tara is a past president of Romance Writers of America and a seven-time RITA® Award finalist. She has also appeared on TV across the country, including *CBS Sunday Morning*. She supports the National Domestic Violence Hotline. If you need help, please contact 1-800-799-7233.

Books by Tara Taylor Quinn

Harlequin Romantic Suspense

The Coltons of Grave Gulch

Colton's Killer Pursuit

Colton 911: Grand Rapids

Colton 911: Family Defender

Where Secrets are Safe

Her Detective's Secret Intent
Shielded in the Shadows

The Coltons of Mustang Valley

Colton's Lethal Reunion

Visit the Author Profile page at Harlequin.com for more titles.

To the two friends who have been with me at the computer, sustaining me this past year: Cinci Davis and Ali Williams. You are my blessings.

Chapter 1

The cold was just about freezing her nose off. Two seconds out of the grocery store and Everleigh could already feel the sting through her jeans and thick black coat. Pushing her overflowing cart—as it turned out, spending two months in prison meant most everything left in her kitchen had to be replaced—she got a wheel caught on a chunk of ice. Pushed harder and skidded over it.

Of course, frozen February *would* be the time she'd be replenishing. Couldn't be summer, when the long trek to the far end of the lot could have been less miserable.

It wasn't like she'd had any warning, any time to prepare for an absence. One minute she'd been waiting tables at Howlin' Eddie's, trying like hell to make enough money to pay the bills, maybe buy some Christmas presents, and the next she'd been handcuffed in front of her coworkers and a couple dozen customers. Accused of murdering her soon-to-be ex-husband.

At the point she'd been arrested, she hadn't even seen Fritz in over a week. He'd moved out the month before. He'd been accusing her of cheating on him, when the truth was, he'd been doing other women behind her back for years. Chump that she was, she'd trusted him.

Crunch. Crunch. Her ankle-length zip-up black boots sounded against the ice and salt crystals as she pushed, lifting a hand briefly to resecure her knitted hat over her short hair and freezing ears, still halfway down the pavement from her beat-up old red Park Avenue…a car that reminded her of herself in some ways. Luxury in name only. Except that her old beater of a car used to actually be top-of-the-line. Her beginnings on the east side of town had been anything but.

Still, she'd made it across the wrong side of the tracks, from lower-income housing and basic public school to the upscale part of Grave Gulch. Meeting Fritz, falling in love with the handsome fitness-guru charmer, marrying and buying a home on the west side, *his* side of town…

Crunch and…her boot slid forward on a patch of ice. With one hand flailing and her heart in her throat, Everleigh gripped her cart harder, lurching against it as she managed to avoid falling on her butt on the pavement. But the sudden movement knocked the bag of baking goods, flour, sugar and chocolate chips out of her cart and onto the wet ground.

Blinking back tears, she bent to rebag her goods. Stupid to cry. She didn't need frozen eyelashes, or reason for her nose to run any more than it already was. The plastic handle on the bag ripped when she put the flour back inside. Her fault. She'd known she should have double bagged it. And really, she'd never been one to cry over spilled milk.

Or baking goods, as was the case here.

The tears that hadn't quite stopped weren't because of her groceries. She knew that. It was just… *everything.* The buildup of two months' worth of sitting in prison twenty minutes from home, awaiting a trial for a murder she hadn't committed while her little house sat empty.

But even that didn't cause emotional overflow. No, the tears were for her gram. Every waking second of the forty-eight hours she'd been out of prison, she'd been mourning for her eighty-year-old role model, heroine, example and fount of love. In an act of desperation, her grandma, Hannah McPherson, had kidnapped a police sketch artist's child just to get leverage so the cops would reinvestigate Fritz's murder.

Gram had been so certain that Everleigh hadn't killed her husband—which she hadn't—that she'd been willing to risk her own freedom to get someone to prove it. Gram had been the only one who'd believed Everleigh hadn't committed the crime.

Hard to believe…thirty-eight years of living in Grave Gulch, on both sides of the tracks…her entire life…caring for people, trying to be kind, doing her best…and everyone, her own mother and aunt included, believed her capable of murder—and that she was guilty!

And now the one person who'd been there for her, unconditionally, her entire life, was sitting in prison. Because while Gram's goal had been met—the police had taken another look at her case and found that their own forensic scientist had tampered with evidence and Everleigh had been exonerated—her grandmother had committed a felony by taking that sweet baby boy. Didn't matter that she'd cared for him lovingly during the few hours he'd been a guest at her home. She'd kidnapped a child. The little cousin of the chief of police.

And still, bottom line, she was a kidnapper, was sitting in prison facing felony charges, and there was nothing Everleigh could do to get her out.

Because while Everleigh hadn't been guilty, Gram was...

Placing her groceries back in the ripped bag, Everleigh blinked through her tears to be able to see well enough to find two ends of plastic to tie together and get the bag back up to her cart, then lodged it securely among the dozen or so other packages still there. Frozen fingers having made the task that much more difficult, she pushed her cart as quickly as she could toward her sorry old car.

Murder or not, Everleigh would rather be the one facing another night in a cell than her grandma. Prison was no place for an eighty-year-old woman with frail bones and a heart filled with love.

She'd thought maybe, with the fault lying in the police department, and the boy's mother being willing to not press charges, Gram would be free. But the DA still charged her.

And it wasn't like Everleigh had any sway with the upper-echelon politicians in town.

Still...she was almost at her car, thank God...there were always silver linings if you looked for them, as Gram had always said. She might not have any pull in town, but Gram did. There'd been Free Granny posters going up all over town. There'd even been a formal protest going on when Everleigh had been released from prison two days before.

And they were still going on downtown every day, outside the police station.

Maybe... *Oommfff.* Someone—or something—slammed into her.

Hands ripped from the basket of her cart with the force that hit her, Everleigh seemed to fly, her feet off the ground, for a brief second before she landed with a thump on top of a heavily coated body much larger than hers. The gloved hands caught her around the waist like a football, held her in place for a brief second and then, just as quickly, let her go.

She looked up just in time to see the back of her car swiped by the front bumper of an old vehicle that hadn't even bothered to stop.

What the hell!

Scrambling to her feet, heart pounding and her breath blowing out steam in large poofs, she saw her basket of groceries rolling off in the distance. And saw the man who'd just tackled her to the ground running after them. Almost starting to cry again as he caught the basket just before it bashed into a light post and pulled it safely back to her.

"We need to call the police," he said, steam vaporizing around his face as he pulled out his phone.

And she recognized him. Had seen him around the police station and in court, too, as she'd arrived for the third day of her trial and found herself released instead. Clarke Colton. And of course, he'd want to call the police, being the big brother to the chief and all.

Plus, he worked for them. As a contracted private investigator.

The thought of police anywhere in her vicinity made her shake worse than the frigid temperatures.

"Someone just tried to run you down," he said, phone to his ear.

Yeah, she'd gotten that. Just hadn't processed it yet.

Clarke Colton spoke into the phone without introducing himself, reporting what he'd just seen happen to her, giving way more of a description of the car than she'd been able to make out, along with the fact that there'd been no license plate on it. His description of the driver followed but wasn't nearly as detailed. With the bulky coat, big gloves and ski mask the person had been wearing, he hadn't even been able to tell if it was male or female. Or any kind of hair color, skin color or body build.

So great, a phantom was after her now? She started to load her groceries with muscles weakened by shock. Fear hadn't set in yet, but she knew it was on its way. She could feel it coming. As soon as she thawed out a bit more.

Why would anyone want to hurt her?

But…someone already had. The missing police-department forensic guy, something-or-other Bowe, who'd tampered with the evidence in her case to make her look guilty. She'd never even met the guy. Had no idea why he'd be out to get her.

But apparently, he still was and…

Clarke dropped his phone in his coat pocket and picked up a couple of her bags of groceries, depositing them in her slightly more dented trunk. The car sure didn't show her in her best light, but from what she understood, Clarke already knew way more about her than she ever cared to know about him. He'd been the one to take another look at her case when Gram kidnapped his cousin.

He'd also been the one who'd found the discrepancy in evidence that had ultimately proved her innocence.

Everleigh might be from the wrong side of the tracks, but Gram had made certain she had her manners. "I owe you a debt of gratitude," she told him. *Just get the bags in the trunk.*

Then she could lock herself in her car and cry. Or drive somewhere safe.

Somewhere she could hide until she could figure out what to do next.

No place that fit that description was coming to her.

She sure as heck wasn't going to her parents' house. They'd believed she was a murderer…

"You don't owe me anything." He loaded the last three bags.

"First you help find the evidence that gets me out of jail, and now this…" She nodded toward the dent in her trunk. "If you hadn't moved when you did, I'd have been smashed between my car and the one..."

Her teeth chattered. She wanted it to be a result of the cold. But it wasn't.

Oh, God. She'd almost been smashed to death!

Suddenly, standing out there on the pavement, in broad daylight, visible to anyone, didn't seem prudent.

Ducking her head, she made her way to the driver's door of her car. Thankfully didn't have to bother unlocking it. The lock had busted a couple of months before. Once inside, she squinted up at her rescuer veiled in the sunshine. Standing between her and the door as he was, he'd left her little choice.

"I'm going to follow you home," he told her. Didn't ask. Told. "Just to make certain you get there safely."

With a nod, she agreed to wait until he came around in his SUV before driving off. Only because he was fulfilling her goal. To get her somewhere safely.

And maybe because, after months of being afraid and alone, falsely accused and powerless, it felt good to have someone at her back.

Not that she'd trust a Colton. Or anyone but Gram. She'd learned that lesson hard and clear.

Just as she knew that the idea of being safe was only a mirage. Home, the scene of a murder two months before, definitely wasn't it. But at the moment, it was all she had.

And...she had groceries to put away. No way could she afford to let all that food spoil.

Oh, God. Had she really almost been killed?

It just didn't make sense.

Nor did the fact that she was a widow, not a divorcée. Fritz *dead*?

But then, since her husband had walked out on her, spreading rumors that she'd been unfaithful to him, nothing had made much sense.

And with Gram in jail…she was beginning to wonder if it ever would again.

Clarke hadn't intended to follow Everleigh Emerson. He'd just been grabbing some bacon from the grocery store. But he'd watched her once he'd caught sight of her. She'd been pushing her cart slowly down aisle seven, moving aside and waiting as an older couple made a spaghetti-sauce choice. And she'd helped a pregnant woman lift a case of bottled water, too.

And if he'd been pressed, he'd have admitted that he'd hung around, waiting to watch her leave, thinking he might have a word with her in the parking lot. Unofficially. As a PI, he hadn't been directed to pursue her case any further, but having delved into the woman's life, he was intrigued by her vagaries.

And as a professional, he wanted to know why Randall Bowe had tampered with evidence on multiple cases, including hers. Did he have something against her specifically? Did the other cases he'd manipulated have anything in common with hers?

Work was life, so sue him if he took it to the grocery store with him.

As it turned out, his dedication to the job, his natural curiosity that made him good at his work, had saved a life that morning.

Following the woman to her small house in a nice

neighborhood on the west side of town, thinking of her raw beginnings, and the way her husband framed her for infidelity to hide his own extramarital affairs, playing on her coming from the wrong side of the tracks and working as a barmaid, to protect his own reputation… he wanted to make certain that she stayed safe. It was just the right thing to do after everything that had happened. Police-department error had put her in prison. The Coltons and the rest of the department owed it to her to help her get her life back.

And, okay, he had to know who'd just tried to run her down. And why.

All of the cops, including those in his family, would be on it officially. Because of the stickiness of the case, the smirch Randall Bowe had put on the police department in general, and because some of the town's residents were starting to get vocal about their mistrust, he'd called the chief of police herself to report Everleigh's grocery-store incident. The chief of police just happened to be his younger sister, Melissa. She was already sending their cousin Grace, a rookie cop, out to canvass streets for any sight of the car.

But as a private investigator, even one who occasionally worked for GGPD, he didn't have to worry about following as many protocols. Something he'd never been all that good at. Which was why the job fit him so well.

Everleigh pulled straight into the garage, leaving the newly shoveled driveway open for him. Or so he thought to himself as he parked behind her.

Though the yard was covered with the snow that had fallen the night before, he figured her for the type to have flower beds lining the front of her house, with colorful blooms all spring. And she'd probably be growing tomatoes in a little garden out back, too.

And she'd come up with all different things to do with them, various ways to prepare them so not a single one went to waste.

At least that was his profile of her based on the testimonies he'd read in her file—from those who knew her.

With a couple of long strides, he was beside her, managing most of the bags there on his own. His muscles and long limbs came in handy for all kinds of things.

"I can get those," she told him, but he didn't listen.

That was a fault his sister pointed out to him on occasion. He always thought he knew best.

He knew what pissed her off was that he so often did. Probably because for so long he'd been more wayward than reliable. A product of their artist mother's genes, he'd decided. He had a spirit that craved freedom.

And what made Melissa love him, he'd also decided, was that he'd learned how to admit when he was wrong. To apologize. And to make good on his debts.

Exploits that didn't exactly pull off as envisioned tended to teach a guy a thing or two.

Moving a little more quickly than the slender model-perfect short-haired blonde woman in front of him, Clarke almost crashed into her as he took the one step up to enter the door she'd just unlocked.

"Oh, my God!" Her cry caught at him, more than the situation would normally have caused.

She was tall, but he was taller; he could easily see beyond her shoulder as she stood stock-still, grocery bags in her hand.

Either she was one hell of a bad housekeeper—which his picture of her didn't relay—or someone had ransacked her house. The hall he could see was strewn with debris. Papers, outerwear, a broken vase with silk flowers askew.

"Step back." All business, he moved quickly, getting in front of her, setting his bags down on the floor and reaching for his gun. "Stay here."

He entered the kitchen. Cupboards were hanging open, things pulled from them onto the floor and counters. As he made his way through the house, he found the same in the living room… Things had been pulled out of spaces; cushions were overturned. Rapidly making his way through the rest of the home, he ascertained, first and foremost, that they were alone.

Whoever had been there had left.

And he had a self-professed job to do—find out who was after Everleigh…and protect her at all costs.

Chapter 2

Everleigh unbuttoned her coat. She had to sit down.

And was afraid to touch anything, not even to pull out one of the four chairs around the kitchen table. Her home, having undergone crime-scene tape, body removal, forensics and then a thorough cleaning, had, just two months later, become the scene of another crime.

Forester! Was he okay? Glancing toward the archway leading from the kitchen to the rest of the house, she told herself that the cat Fritz had brought home a month before he'd walked out on her would be tucked safely under her bed, where he spent most of his time.

That was apparently where he'd been found after Fritz's murder and her subsequent arrest.

Standing there, trembling, she surveyed the mess,

hearing Clarke Colton moving about the house, listening for signs of struggle and feeling a need to dial 911.

Refusing to allow herself to become overwhelmed.

She couldn't put away groceries until she cleaned up the mess all over the cupboards and counters, which were now part of a crime scene.

Her milk was going to spoil.

No. The refrigerator hadn't been touched. Glomming on to having something constructive to do, to help her keep her sanity, she shrugged out of her coat, quickly found the bags with frozen and refrigerated items. She put them all on their proper shelves and in their proper drawers in the side-by-side refrigerator Fritz had bought her for Christmas ten years before.

Back when his business had been doing well. He'd been on top of the world then—and on top of other women, too, as it had turned out, but she hadn't known that then. She'd thought their marriage healthy enough. Was somewhat disenchanted with what it had turned out to be—all about Fritz, rather than the partnership they'd vowed to give each other—but had been giving it her all. Determined to make it work. Had been focused on starting a family…

Before she'd unloaded one full bag of perishables, Clarke came around the corner, his gun back in the holster at his waist. And his phone to his ear.

"Yeah, Melissa, it's me again. The Emerson home has been completely ransacked. Break-in was a bedroom window, not the master. No sign of the perp. My guess is whoever did this is the same person who just tried to run her over…"

Silence and then, "Yeah."

More silence. Watching him, instead of surveying the mess, calmed her. He had blue eyes.

"Yeah."

He was a Colton. And from what she'd heard, a womanizer like Fritz. She was grateful for his help. But wanted him gone.

"I'm on it." He hung up. Glanced at her with obvious compassion.

She'd fallen for a charmer once. Clarke could turn that warm, caring glance on someone else. She'd have her own back from there on out, thank you very much.

"Troy's on his way over," he said. "My cousin Detective Troy Colton."

Yeah, she knew who he was.

The man who'd come into her place of employment and slapped handcuffs on her wrists. She'd never, ever forget that feel of cold hard steel clamping down against her wrist bone. Bruising it.

Right now, she had to get her head out of shock city and deal with the current situation.

"Someone evidently wants me dead," she said. "And they tear up my house..." They were definitely out to get her...*still*. The same fact she'd been living with the two long months she'd been sitting in prison. "I don't get it," she continued. "Unless this has something to do with why Randall Bowe framed me in the first place..."

She'd never even met the department's forensic scientist. Had no idea why he'd have it in for her.

"Doubtful," Clarke said. "Yours wasn't the only case he tampered with."

She nodded. But... "I've heard he's on the run," she

said, not able to let it go. When a guy you've never met lands you in prison and you're facing the rest of your life locked up in a cell… "Until we know why he did what he did, we don't know he's not behind this." Shuddering, she shut up. No good was going to come out of scaring herself. She needed her wits about her. And the strength Gram had instilled within her from a very early age.

Taking care of her was her job. No one else's.

"He's on the run because he knows we're on to him," Clarke told her, still standing in the entryway to the kitchen, as though purposefully blocking her from the rest of the house. And seemingly willing to stand there and chat for the rest of the day.

The man had some age on him, but then, at thirty-eight, so did she.

Age gave him a maturity she found…reassuring. And he was way too good-looking, all tall and muscular with thick brown hair and blue eyes that seemed to see inside her. He wore his sexuality as confidently as he did the tight jeans that hugged his…hips…well enough to be on the front cover of a magazine.

He'd unbuttoned his thick corduroy coat, revealing a blue plaid flannel shirt across a far-too-impressive expanse of muscular chest.

What in the hell was the matter with her? She'd spent two months in prison, not twenty years locked away from all men. And she'd never been one to ogle a guy, anyway.

Had to be the tension.

He was a distraction. That was all.

She couldn't clean yet. Not until Troy, Clarke and the others released her home back to her a second time.

"Bowe isn't going to risk getting caught by running people down in the middle of town. He's facing way too many charges to take a chance on that. And while he might not have gotten the conviction he wanted where you were concerned, he did get them for others."

Shuddering again, she felt for whoever those people were. She'd come so close to being one of them.

When the thought of the cell brought a jittering sense of panic, she forced her mind back to the moment at hand.

Which was equally scary. Just in a different way.

It made sense that Bowe would not be the one after her now. Besides, why ransack her home if he intended to kill her? "So, who would be? And what were they looking for here?" Why ransack her house just to scare her and then go try to run her down? She'd never have known about the vandalism to her things if she'd been killed. Which meant…

"Whoever was here was looking for something," she said slowly.

Clarke nodded.

She looked up at him. "And they want me dead, too."

"Which leads me to believe that today's events are connected to Fritz's murder. Most likely, the real killer is behind it. Fritz had something that person wanted."

"Based on the fact that whoever it was came for me, after ransacking the house, do we think he or she found what it was? Or not?"

Shaking his head, Clarke took a step closer to her,

but when she stepped back, he stopped immediately. He got kudos for that.

And a shard of fear of an entirely different kind shot through her and she frowned. "Wait. There've been a few times since I got home that I've thought someone else has been in the house." She started out slowly, but her words picked up pace as reality set in further. "The first thing I did when I got home two days ago, after getting Forester home, was put everything back in its usual place. The house had been cleaned professionally, but no one but me would know where things went. But then it seemed like things were moved again. I put it down to my having missed them the other day. I was a bit…distracted…" Worried sick about her grandmother was more like it. "Then I noticed closet doors open, but I put that down to me being paranoid. Figuring they'd been opened when the police went through here scouring for evidence or something."

His attention seemed to sharpen and focus completely on her. His look was intent.

Could it be that a killer had been in her home the same time she'd been there?

The idea was creepy as well as frightening.

Scary beyond what she felt equipped to handle. So, she had to find more strength than she knew was there. Draw on an empty well until it sprang new sources…

She continued, "Last night…I was certain I heard someone in the house, a couple of times. I really had a sense that I wasn't alone. But then Forester jumped up on my bed, and I chalked the sensations up to him. He'd only been here a few months before I went to prison, and he generally spends most of his time under my bed when I'm around…"

Speaking of which…now that she knew the house was clear of any immediate danger…she brushed past Clarke, careful to keep as much distance as the cupboards on either side of her allowed, and headed to the third and largest of the house's three bedrooms. The purple coverlet she'd left neatly on the bed that morning was in a lump on the floor. She couldn't even assess the rest of the mess and damage.

Things didn't matter as much as life…

On her knees and then hunched down, she peeked under the bed. And came eyeball to eyeball with the cat who never quite seemed to trust her.

"Hey, Forester," she said softly. "Did you see who was here, buddy? Can you tell me who it was?" Of course, she knew there'd be no reply, but she'd been working on the hope that if she used a gentle voice and real conversation, the cat would begin to trust her.

She didn't blame him when it didn't happen. She wasn't going to be sweet-talked into trusting again, either.

Not ever.

Everleigh Emerson sure was prickly. Scared as hell, too, if he read the expressions flittering across her face right—and he usually did read other people pretty accurately—and yet putting up "leave me alone, I don't need help" signals all over the place. Which made the promise he'd just made to his sister a bit more challenging to keep.

Another challenge loomed, as well…that curvaceous

backside in those jeans, the zipped-up black leather ankle boots drawing attention to long legs bent under her as she peered at her cat… He couldn't afford to be attracted to this woman.

Not on any level.

All too aware that they were in the room where she'd later be sleeping, without those jeans and boots, he headed out of the room the second she stood up. Kept his back to her for a second as he gave parts of himself a stern talking-to, and then stepped aside to let her lead him back out to the rest of the house.

She'd had very little control of her life, for what sounded like a lot longer than the time she'd spent locked up.

He didn't want to take away any more of it than he absolutely had to, to keep her safe.

"You don't have to stay," Everleigh said, coming to a stop at the archway leading into the ravaged living area with a view of the small, equally pillaged den just beyond it. "I'm fine to wait for your cousin on my own."

Was he mistaken or had there been a slight emphasis on the words *your cousin*? Not that he blamed her if there had been.

Some of the town's residents were having a hard time trusting their police department at the moment after what Bowe had done. But he knew that most of the cops, Coltons and non-Coltons alike, were hardworking, capable and honest people who'd dedicated their lives to police work. His family, in particular, had grown up in the shadow of his aunt's senseless and unsolved home-invasion murder. The incident was so much a part of their family it had literally shaped who they all were, instilled in them a deep understanding of the need for justice—most particularly for her kids, Clarke's cousins.

His own lack of regard for rules, and early penchant for flouting convention, was a part of that, too, he supposed, which was why he was a PI, not a cop like so many of them. There'd been such a tight rein on all of them growing up…or so it had seemed to him, anyway. He'd needed to break out of the box. To do things his own way, whether his way was best, smartest, safest—or not. Not all of his family members would concur with the sense of tight reins on them, he was sure. It wasn't something they sat around and talked about.

Regardless of who his family was, or how many of them worked for the GGPD, the truth was, people in town had a valid reason for mistrusting GGPD at the moment. One of their own had violated that trust in the most heinous way.

Randall Bowe had one hell of a lot to answer for. He was going to wish he'd never done anything to sic Clarke Colton on him, that was for sure.

But first things first…

"I…uh…don't want to impose on you, but…since I was the one who found the evidence that set you free…I was hoping you'd trust me enough to help you find out who's behind all of this…" He spread his arm wide to encompass the disaster of a mess in her home.

The way she was assessing him, he braced for a kindly worded slap in the face.

"I'm not just a private investigator," he told her.

"I work for the GGPD regularly. You can check up on me."

He was going to have to find a way to get her to agree to him protecting her, in order to have any hope of getting her to comply with what Melissa wanted.

What he must want, too, since he'd agreed to his little sister's suggestion without even a token argument. And if she tried to make anything of that, she'd get double the argument from him.

"I was hoping life was going to get back to normal." She looked around her. "A new normal," she amended.

"It will." He wanted that for her. With a strength of emotion that rattled him. What the hell? She was a case. He was doing a favor for his sister. For the whole Colton family. This was not his own personal crusade. "This whole episode, though, starting with your husband being murdered… It's just not done yet. Let me help you finish it."

"Okay." He almost took a step back, he was so surprised by her capitulation. "But only because I don't trust the GGPD to do the job themselves. And because I can afford to pay you," she added. "Here I am, two days ago, worried about getting a proper haircut, and I hear that I'm receiving a payout from Fritz's life insurance. Since he didn't file for divorce yet, and didn't change the beneficiary, I'm it. I go down on Tuesday to sign papers and then the money will be direct deposited into my account, at which point I can pay you. Ironic, isn't it? He pilfers away everything either of us earned, leaves me and then ends up leaving me well-off. Which just makes me look guilty for killing him, doesn't it?"

His gut lurched at the instant fear that emanated

from her hazel-eyed gaze. "You've been exonerated, Everleigh," he reminded her softly.

She nodded. "I didn't even know he'd kept the life-insurance policy…until two days ago."

"So, you got your haircut," he blurted inanely, wanting to bring her back from that brink of fear. And then realizing that talking to her about her appearance probably wasn't the way to get her to agree to his next request.

When her hand went immediately to her short, sexily ruffled, perky blond cut, and then almost immediately dropped self-consciously, he wished he'd left them at life insurance.

Tried to fix that with, "You don't need to pay me." What he wanted from her was her trust. And that was something he was going to have to earn, first.

He wasn't a novice at that particular situation. After the exploits of his twenties and early thirties, disappearing for days at a time on some challenge, adventure or case, without checking in, he'd spent a lot of time earning back the trust of his family members. Melissa's request that he protect Everleigh Emerson, just until they could figure out what was going on, was a huge sign of the trust he'd earned back.

And part of the reason why he'd agreed so readily to do so.

Part of the reason… The other part was standing in front of him, frowning again.

"I don't want your money."

The words didn't help. If anything, they made the situation worse.

"The GGPD owes you."

She nodded, and he breathed out a sigh of relief as the third try got him out of hot water. Momentarily, at least.

"I don't want to scare you, but I think it's pretty obvious that you aren't safe here…" He glanced around them and then back at her. "And based on what happened at the grocery store, you might not be safe in town, either. So, what I'm proposing, first and foremost, is that you…"

"I'm not leaving town. Not with Gram still in jail. No way." The adamant shake of her head, the way her hair bounced, distracted him for a second.

"I was going to suggest… In truth, my sister, Chief Colton, advised me to suggest I help keep you safe. I'd be happy for you to temporarily move into my guest room," he told her. "It's there specifically for the use of anyone my family needs to house. As your newly appointed personal private investigator, I'm advising you to accept this invitation. Just for a few days. Maybe less. Give us time to find out who's behind the incident at the grocery store this morning. And the break-in."

"I've got my family…my mom… I can stay with her…" She frowned again. "But…I don't want to put them in danger…"

He pounced. "Exactly. I'm armed. And trained."

"I'm also still dealing with the fact that they all turned on me, believing I'd actually murdered Fritz… I love them, but I'd rather not stay there, not with dealing with this, too…still… I'm not going to put you out because your sister orders you to…"

"Hey." He cut her off right there. "Police chief or not, she's my *little* sister, and she doesn't order me to do anything. She thought it would be a good idea for me to help you out. I offered for you to stay at my place." He took a breath, surprised at the tension tightening his chest as he waited for her response. "She claims that I have a tendency to speak my opinions as though I'm always right and leave little room for others to disagree."

"Do you?"

He shrugged. "Not as much as I used to. But I don't often say something unless I've looked at the situation and have reason to believe I'm correct. And I've learned to trust my gut. It generally steers me right."

But maybe not about this. What was he doing inviting this woman into his home? Just the two of them. Alone. With her being so gut-wrenchingly a…turn-on…and him…noticing that?

"Okay."

"Okay?"

"Okay, I'll stay in your guest room."

Wow. He'd gotten off easy on that one. "You should get some stuff together—let us get out of here before Troy and his crew take over the place…" He wanted to get her out of there before she changed her mind. He wasn't telling her, but he was in no doubt whatsoever that her life was in real danger.

Anyone who'd try to run down a person in a grocery-store parking lot in broad daylight in the middle of downtown wasn't going to just go away. Or follow any kind of logic, either.

"Is the idea to leave my car here?"

She caught on quick. The beater would be easily recognizable. "Yes."

"Then I have a favor to ask..."

Whatever she needed...he was officially at her disposal.

"I need to see my grandmother. I'm worried about her spending too much time without seeing a loved one... She thrives on family and..."

That wouldn't even be a favor. It was a given. "Of course," he told her. "I'll call ahead to make sure that she'll be available for a private visit with you..."

Because there were times when knowing the police chief's brother in Grave Gulch came with perks—not a price to pay.

Chapter 3

He didn't want her money. How did you trust a guy who wanted you to believe he was asking nothing from you? Women the world over knew that if a guy didn't want your money, he most likely wanted something else.

Her money was all he was going to get.

Didn't matter if he billed her or not, she would pay him. Everleigh had spent too many years of her life forced to take what others were willing to part with and to be grateful for it.

She wasn't doing it again. Life had exacted too much from her already. She wasn't giving away any more of her pride.

Before she packed, Clarke asked her to take a look around to determine if she noticed anything missing, paying particular attention to any place where there might have been valuables. From what she could tell, nothing had been taken. Not even the wedding and engagement rings she'd had in her jewelry box. None of the jewelry, most of it costume variety, had been disturbed.

After calling the neighbor who'd watched Forester while she'd been in prison, she got the cat out from under the bed with only a minimal scratch and saw him safely housed next door, had a bag packed and was sitting in the front seat of Clarke's navy blue SUV twenty minutes after she'd accepted his offer of help.

Troy Colton had arrived while she'd been packing, and Clarke had handled that aspect for her. She'd never even had to speak with the detective. Clarke had earned some of his fee right there. And a tad bit of gratitude, as well.

Still, sitting there in his car with her suitcase in the back, bundled up in her thick black coat, she was almost overwhelmed with trepidation. What was she doing moving in with a man she'd known only a couple of hours?

Not moving in with him, of course. She was going into protective custody in a guest room of a licensed, armed and trained professional investigator and under the watchful eyes of the chief of police.

And she needed to get on top of the morning's events. Not let them control her.

"I guess this is kind of odd, asking you to take me to visit the woman who kidnapped your cousin." Gram had kidnapped the toddler from a wedding where the entire Grave Gulch police department was in attendance, but not with the intention to hurt the child. There'd never been a threat to that baby's life.

"She took drastic measures to get us to see what was right under our own eyes," Clarke said, not taking his gaze from the road and the world outside the vehicle. He seemed to scan everything at once. Constantly. Moving his head little, but his gaze a lot. Intently.

She'd hate to be a bug under his microscope.

And appreciated his honesty where her grandmother was concerned. Still, Gram's drastic measure… wow…so drastic. She'd broken the law in a way that couldn't be ignored. You couldn't just kidnap someone anytime injustice was done. The action had helped eventually exonerate Everleigh—but it was still inexcusable.

"She would never have hurt Danny."

"I know."

Okay, then. That conversation was done. They had fifteen minutes to go until they got to the prison.

Time for her to figure out who wanted her dead? Who'd vandalized her home with so much rage?

All she got was blankness. No one, other than maybe Fritz, had ever thrown that kind of anger in her direction… How did she find a demon with no suspects?

"Hannah apparently loves you an awful lot." His words pulled her thoughts back from the dark abyss, and it took her a second to realize he was still talking about Gram.

"I know. And I love her the same. I can't let her just spend the rest of her life in prison. There has to be something I can do…" She'd trade places with her if she could, if the law would allow such a thing. She glanced at Clarke. "Or maybe, instead of you working for me, there's something you could do?" She couldn't think of it at the moment.

"I could talk to her, if you'd like. Try to convince her to take a plea deal so that the case doesn't go to trial. Once a jury and judge get it, there are laws that dictate their choices and her sentencing..."

Heavy weight settled over her as she listened to him. She knew full well how the legal system worked. Knew that she'd been days from a life sentence herself, in a trial that hadn't been going at all in her favor, when Gram's bold move had turned the tide for her.

So, what bold move could she make to save Gram? The townspeople were still holding protests. She'd seen a group of them on the courthouse steps depicted on the news that morning.

But the law was the law. Those in charge had to uphold it or risk going to jail themselves.

"Can I take a rain check on that?" she asked Clarke. "I'd like to talk to her first, to see what I can do..."

"I'm fairly certain that if she'd take a plea agreement, the DA's office would be willing to offer some kind of sentence that doesn't have her dying in jail."

"If she lives long enough, you mean." Ten years in prison would make Gram ninety when she got out. Ten years in prison would kill her.

He shrugged. And Everleigh wasn't happy to have won the point. Nor was she happy with any other options where her grandmother was concerned. An insanity plea might hold some weight—except that Gram was as sharp as they came and wouldn't be willing to sacrifice her cognitive freedom to get out of paying for what she'd done.

And there was the crux of it...

"Gram's a stickler for accountability," she said, tears pushing at her. She pushed back, and won, but the profound sadness that had ignited them lingered. "No way she'd be right with walking away from a crime she committed," she continued. Because it was important all of a sudden that he know that, in spite of her impoverished background and having a family who'd all—except for Gram—accepted her guilt when presented with DNA evidence, she came from some good stock. "She knew when she made the choice to take that baby that there'd be a price to pay."

It was she who was struggling with her grandmother paying it. Not Gram. They were on the outskirts of prison real estate and her stomach tightened to the point of pain. Two days ago, she'd woken up within those walls.

Being caged up, losing all of her freedoms... Those months were going to haunt her for the rest of her life.

She couldn't let Gram end her life that way. "I'll talk to her about the plea agreement," she said out loud.

"There are mitigating circumstances here. The fact that she didn't hurt the baby, in fact, loved him well during the hours he was in her home, that she never even threatened to harm him, that she'd tried to get someone to look at your case through all normal channels, that his mother doesn't want to press charges... By law, all of that allows the DA to offer a plea agreement that would be much more in her favor," Clarke said, as though he was on Gram's side.

And, though her guard didn't come down where he was concerned, that comment did have her softening toward him a little bit.

At Everleigh's request that he not accompany her to see her grandmother, Clarke waited for her out in the parking lot. It meant he had to turn the vehicle on a few times to keep warm, but he wasn't keen on hanging out in prison reception.

The Free Granny protesters were out in full force, in spite of the cold, lined up along the wall with their signs, warming their gloved hands over disposable coffee cups. Melissa had told him that the group was being well run, with everyone serving shifts and stationed outside the GGPD and the prison. They also had a quickly growing social-media presence.

Where they needed to be was outside the DA's office.

And even then…did they really want to have a society run by herd justice, as opposed to laws? If it were up to him, Hannah McPherson wouldn't have spent one minute in jail, but you couldn't just let a kidnapper go free because you understood their motive.

The ramifications of that… What if anytime anyone felt their cause justified, they just broke the law?

Where had all the protesters been when Everleigh was in prison? If more had raised a fuss to free her, maybe Bowe's wrongdoings would have been found out sooner. Everleigh had proclaimed her innocence from the beginning, but no one had listened.

Except for Hannah McPherson.

But then she'd broken the law. She didn't proclaim

her innocence. They'd found the toddler in her home. And *now* protesters got involved?

The time in the car gave him a chance to formulate a plan of investigation. He'd started his early February Thursday morning expecting to be pursuing the Randall Bowe case. Instead, Troy would be taking a lead on that, and while he'd still be helping, his first priority now was Everleigh Emerson. Keeping her safe. And finding out who wanted her dead.

With a constant watch on the prison door, just in case she didn't text him that she was on her way out as he'd instructed so he could pick her up at the curb, he took out the little notebook and pen from his inner coat pocket and started jotting notes.

Questions for Everleigh mostly.

Maybe whoever was after her had nothing to do with her husband's killer, but his instincts were telling him the murder and subsequent murder attempt were connected.

Could be someone had wanted both her and Fritz dead. Someone who benefited from them both being gone before their divorce was final, maybe? But then, why not kill her off, too? Before she was sent to jail?

Who would such a beneficiary be? They had no children. She'd mentioned life insurance… Did they have a joint policy? He jotted another question.

And his text-message alert sounded. She was ready.

And so was he. Ready to get to work on her case.

But first…

"How'd it go?" he asked, trying to assess her expression as she climbed quickly back in beside him, waving as the protesters cheered her. The waft of floral perfume that came with her distracted him.

She shrugged. Stared out the front window. Taking her cue, he drove off the premises. And then asked, "What did she say about the plea-agreement angle?"

"That she'd think about it."

Could mean so many things. "Do you think she will really consider it?" Or had it been a polite blow-off? How could anyone choose to spend more time in jail than necessary?

"Yes. She wouldn't tell me she'd do something and then not do it."

But still, Everleigh was clearly upset. If anyone had hurt the eighty-year-old woman…

"How was she doing?"

With a grimace, Everleigh glanced at him, her eyes moist, though there were no visible tears. "Better than I am," she told him. "She's in good spirits, really. Proud of herself for getting me out. For helping to prove my innocence. She wants me to be happy about it, too, and while I'm relieved to the point of light-headedness at being exonerated, not at the cost of her being in prison…"

It was almost as though he could feel her pain. The helplessness of knowing that someone was suffering as a result of caring for you, and there was nothing you could do to help them. He'd felt a bit of the same in the recent breakup nightmare. If he'd had any idea the woman had wanted a life with him, he'd never have asked her out once, let alone multiple times.

"She's being treated okay?"

"Yeah. As far as I can tell. Gram's feisty. She looks and acts younger than she is. It's just…seeing her in that jumpsuit…" She shook her head, glanced out her side-door window.

There was nothing he could do. His job was to drive. To find out who was after Everleigh. This woman seemed to care more about her grandmother in a cell than she did about her own life. He didn't know what to make of that kind of selflessness. Sure, he'd die for any of his family… but to grieve over their life circumstances… Maybe he needed to do a bit more in the loving department.

Or maybe he was making far too much of his current client's saddened demeanor.

He was much better and more successful at his job when he could get into the mindset of his clients. That was all he was doing.

He welcomed the reminder. The chance for a return to his own sense of normal.

A way he could be moved by the woman who'd so unexpectedly, and temporarily, entered his life, and not get freaked out about it.

"Melissa made sure that she's being kept with light offenders on a ward that has seen no violence whatsoever," he offered.

She nodded. Whether she'd already known or not, he couldn't tell.

He drove some more.

And reminded himself that he was on the job, not being a friend to a beautiful woman.

"You mentioned your husband's life insurance," he said, thinking of the questions on his list. "Do you have a policy, as well?"

She shook her head. "Fritz didn't want to pay for

both. He said that we needed it just for him to protect his business."

"So that's yours now, too?"

Another shrug. "Yes, but I don't intend to keep it."

So maybe her attacker had something to do with the business? Joint life insurance was out.

"Who would be the beneficiary if you were out of the picture?"

Her gaze was clear as she turned toward him. He only got a brief glimpse of those hazel eyes, because of driving, but as her pain appeared to have subsided for the moment, he felt better. "We didn't specify," she said. "Our mutual will, which would have been made null and void by the divorce, just states that everything that is his goes to me and everything that is mine goes to him, in the event that either of us passes before the other. We made the wills out shortly after we were married on the advice of our pastor. I figured that we'd amend them once we had kids…"

He knew from the case files that she and Fritz had been married almost eighteen years. And wondered why there weren't any kids. Was one or the other of them incapable? Had it just never happened? Did one of them change their mind?

They weren't questions that pertained to his place in her life. So why did he find himself needing the answers?

"Can you think of anyone at the health club who'd benefit from you being gone? Or anything Fritz might have had at home, pertaining to it, that someone could need?"

"No. The club was a failing venture. We own the

building and the equipment, but Fritz was really the biggest asset. He was a great motivator, and was precise and regimented when it came to designing and monitoring individual workouts for his clients..."

He'd done some digging and already knew the club wasn't doing well. But... "If he was that good, why was the business faltering?"

"Because while Fritz excelled at what he did, he didn't spend enough time doing it. He'd rather be having a good time, I now know, with the next good-looking woman who walked in the door. And as he got older, the younger the better, apparently—as long as they were legally adults. Instead of investing money back in the business, or working the hours necessary to keep things going, he worked enough to have money to spend on lavish weekend jaunts with whatever beauty he'd happened to charm."

Clarke had heard some rumors about the man cheating...but nothing to that extent. And with no actual proof to back them up. He hadn't looked for the proof and didn't know if anyone else had done so. But, after just a few hours with Everleigh, he'd begun to doubt their truth—until now. Who'd cheat on a woman like her? One who, in spite of her wrongful incarceration, wasn't filled with hate or bitterness. One who cared more about her grandmother's plight than her own. One who seemed to nurture the air around her.

"I don't get it," he said aloud, when it would have been more prudent to keep his mouth shut.

"Get what?"

"Why he'd do that to you. Did you know?"

The force with which her head turned, shooting

an icy gaze at him, made him wince. Mostly because he knew he deserved the reaction. And because she hadn't deserved the comment.

"I didn't know." She turned to face front again and spoke the words quietly seconds later. Said gently, "I realize I should have known. It happened so gradually. And sometimes I was the woman he took away with him, which was great. And also made me think our marriage was fine, as my husband kept wanting me to go away with him. The other times he left… he'd said he was going to seminars. And that he was invited as a guest artist to teach other trainers. I know sometimes that was true because I went on a few of those with him, too.

"I didn't see the corporate finances, either," she continued after a short silence. "He handled all of that. I dealt with our personal finances, and it wasn't until he was depositing so little of the business earnings in our personal account that I knew something was wrong. I asked him about it, and he said that he'd had to update the club, to buy new equipment to keep up with the technological times. What I hadn't known was that he'd always been making a whole lot more than he shared with me. He did the business taxes separate from our personal ones we filed jointly. And he liked to keep our personal income to a minimum. Said the business could absorb the tax payment that way… I should have kept a better eye on our money."

She was speaking as though to a lawyer, and it dawned on him that it was because she'd done exactly that—just a month before she'd been arrested for murder. Following which, she'd had two months to think about it all. Ad nauseam, he'd guess.

His gut jerked. What had happened to her…it so wasn't right.

"Last year, when I was having trouble making the mortgage payment, I got the job at Howlin' Eddie's and ended up having to keep it to pay the bills. That's when our marriage really started to unravel. Fritz was crazy jealous, hated me in the skimpy barmaid's outfit, started accusing me of nasty things, saying that I liked the chance to flirt with the male customers while they were drinking… It was crazy. He knew I'm not like that. But I know now that he was judging me by his own behavior."

Clarke needed the information she was giving him. But he could feel himself struggling not to hit something as he took it in. The woman had been a faithful, loving wife. Trust shouldn't be abused that way. And, still, he had to ask the obvious question. Because he had to understand how the life she'd led could somehow be coming back to bite her in the ass.

"Why not get a job at the grocery store?"

"Waitressing pays a lot better, especially at a place like Howlin' Eddie's, or any place where there's a good crowd and alcohol being served. And there are tips. I needed money fast. And I waited tables all through high school and during the two years I spent at community college, too, which is where I met Fritz, by the way. I was taking business classes, hoping to open my own hair salon someday, and Fritz was finishing up some advanced training class. I'd gone to the gym between classes and heading to the diner, to get a workout in, and he was there…"

A woman at the gym he'd charmed. Probably not his first. And definitely not his last. But…

"You must have been different from the rest of Fritz's girlfriends," he said, half to himself. But not quite. From her tone, he could tell she was questioning her choices, wondering how she couldn't have seen… "It sounds like he made a career out of finding sexual playmates in the guise of training at the gym," he expanded, "but when he met you…he wanted more than that."

At least, he hoped that was what it had been. He'd known her only a few hours and could already tell she deserved far more than the creep had given her.

When no comment was forthcoming, he asked another question. One that wasn't on his list… "Why didn't you ever open your salon?"

"Fritz said that we couldn't afford two businesses, and that we didn't need the money, either. He was obviously wrong about that last bit, at least in recent years, with the health club. We'd both said we wanted someone at home, raising our kids, and somehow the years just kept passing by. I was doing a lot of volunteer work, mostly at the community center in the neighborhood where I grew up. We offered everything from meals, childcare, and haircuts on a volunteer basis as we could. And there were socials and sporting events, too. Fritz encouraged me to spend time there. Said we were blessed and had to give back. I'm guessing now that he liked me there because it kept me away from the west side of town and the circles that would know what he was up to. I ended up working there more hours than a full-time job. From writing grants to cooking… He'd go on and on about all the great work I did, with his parents mostly, and I only recently figured out he was using me to cushion his own reputation with them. Just like he claimed that I was cheating as a reason for our divorce, to protect his reputation with them. He didn't want to get written out of their will."

There was bitterness in her tone.

Not nearly as much bitterness as he was feeling on her behalf.

And as he pulled into the garage beneath the high-rise building that housed his two-story condo, he vowed that he was going to do everything in his power to take away the sting Fritz Emerson had administered to his wife.

He'd find out who was after her.

He'd protect her from them.

And he'd see that every single cop in the state visited her salon to get their hair done if she decided she wanted to open one.

She already owned the building. Fritz's health club was in a more affluent area downtown and would be a perfect spot for the type of business she'd talked about. Turning a health club into a salon wouldn't be that much of a stretch…

Yeah, maybe he'd talk to her about the idea. Talk to his lawyer about giving her a cut rate on setting up a corporation. Maybe he'd…

Show her to the guest room and stick to the task he'd been assigned.

Chapter 4

The room he showed her to was quite lovely. A surprise, to be sure, with its rose-and-brown matching decor, in a bachelor pad. The rest of the place was nice, too, just without the rose highlights. Clearly a woman's touch.

A girlfriend, perhaps? The man wasn't married, had a reputation around town, but that didn't mean he wasn't in a serious committed monogamous relationship at the moment. Or, even more likely, more than one relationship, non-monogamous.

And that idea had no business being a disappointment to her. She wanted nothing to do with Clarke Colton's personal life. Didn't want to be associated with his life once she was safe to resume her own.

Whenever *that* was going to be. He'd asked her

about her own life choices, her lack of a long-term career; his doing so had brought back all of the longings she'd put aside over the years. Her volunteer work was necessary and gave vital care to so many in need. She'd truly been blessed and fulfilled working at the center. And had told herself she was selfish wanting more. But she was done playing beta to Fritz's manipulation of her thoughts.

But with Fritz gone, she was going to have to earn a living. While his life insurance was a nice sum, and she did have the health-club building, there was no way she was going to freeload from his demise. Just didn't seem right.

Yet she'd been settling for so long…where did she even begin to carve out a whole new life for herself?

She began by getting herself out of danger. Or helping others more qualified to do so. Clarke had shown her quickly through the condo in a high-rise building. He'd left her at the door of the room she'd be occupying, pointing out its own adjoining private bath, before disappearing. He'd told her that once she was settled, he'd meet her downstairs.

She didn't need to get settled. Wasn't planning to stay long enough to warrant settling in. Unzipping her suitcase, she took out her toiletry bag, scrubbed her face and hands—to remove the smell and feeling of prison air—and then quickly reapplied her normal makeup. Foundation, mascara, a little eye shadow for shading, and she was done. Her fingers were the best comb for her short, sassy windblown hair.

A style choice she'd made in spite of the fact that her hair was the only thing sassy about her.

Or maybe because of it.

And then she ventured downstairs. Not sure where she'd find Clarke. Hoping she didn't have to poke into too much of his private space to find him.

He clearly liked books. There were shelves housing them in just about every room she'd seen, including hers. Fiction, nonfiction...didn't seem to matter.

She wondered if he read any of them, or if, perhaps, the same decorator who'd tended to her room had added the books to soften the more austere lines of the rest of the space.

Admonished herself for wondering. Whether he read or not was none of her business. How good he was at his job was all that mattered to her, and since he and the GGPD had been good enough to get her out of jail when her own attorney hadn't done so, he'd more than proved his professional ability.

She found him sitting behind an impressive solid wood desk in a large room that reached off the spacious living area. Feeling like an interloper, she passed an impressive home theater system with a lovely large TV and knocked on the opened off-white door.

"Yeah." He looked up from an array of computer screens of varying sizes. "Everleigh, come on in. I've just been searching some databases to compare registered employees at the health club over the past five years with criminal records..."

Good. Okay, then. Relaxing some, she walked slowly across the room to a dark leather armchair and little table with a lamp set.

Settling into the chair, her pose as prim as a schoolgirl's, she asked, "Did you find anything suspicious there?"

His raised brow, as he glanced from the screen to her, seemed to hold amusement. He said, "I've only had about ten minutes to look." He grinned.

She almost grinned back. Almost, but not quite. "Sorry."

"Don't be." Pushing a laptop aside, putting them in direct line of vision with each other, he asked if her room was okay.

And for some reason, she replied with, "It's really nice, actually. Comfortable, but calming and peaceful, too. Who decorated it for you?"

"How do you know I didn't do it myself?"

The first thing she noticed was that he didn't deny her assumption. And the second was that he appeared to be baiting her. The third, that she'd kind of liked the way his grin made her stomach flip-flop, kept her from smiling back. "You're right. I apologize," she said, instead of holding tight to her assumption.

"No, you're right. I didn't put that room together. I told you the room is there specifically for guests, free for the use of my siblings in the event of overload, and my sister took over in there."

In there. "So…you did the rest of the place?" Including the books?

His single nod spoke volumes. Looking around her, picturing what she'd seen of his home, she was impressed. And didn't have room for that in her current sphere.

Didn't have room for a flirt in her life ever again.

"So far, I'm finding nothing with your ex-husband's

club that would be a motive for killing him. From what I can see so far, and from what I've seen from case files, witness testimonies indicate that he didn't cheat with married women."

She hadn't known that. Wasn't sure it made a difference, though. He'd cheated. She was glad, though, that the man she'd vowed herself to had at least seemed to have *some* standards...

"So, no angry husbands...and no one who stood to gain by his being dead, in terms of the company's future. As you said, he ran it into the ground. From last year's business registration, it appears that he only had a couple of employees left, and they've both since found other positions."

She hadn't known that, either, being tied up in prison as she'd been. But she was glad to hear it. Relieved that no one else was suffering because of Fritz's self-focused choices.

"Good news is, after a quick look at a financial record also in his file, while he has credit-card debt, it's not substantial, and there's no debt or spending that would point to creditors of a shadier variety."

"Fritz would go to his dad for a loan, if he needed one," she said. "Ron would give him a lecture first, but he'd give Fritz the money. It happened a time or two when he was first starting the gym. No way Fritz would risk dealing with some shady shark. He'd lose his inheritance. The one thing his father expected of him was to uphold the family name."

"Which you don't do by cheating on your wife."

She acknowledged the comment with a nod, accompanied by a sick feeling inside her that he couldn't see. "Hence, his lies about me cheating."

Just like he surely knew that Fritz's body had been found in his small den at their home, having been bashed over the head with a heavy stained-glass paperweight. What he wouldn't know was that she hadn't even been in that room since Fritz had moved out the month before. Not even to clean. That there'd been no way her hair and fibers from her apron could have been found on the murder weapon, which he kept in the den.

She'd told more than one Colton at the time of her arrest—though, from what she'd gathered since, that part of her statement wasn't going to make it into court. And then her attorney had told her not to say any more. Her lawyer's inexperience had nearly cost her the rest of her life.

Until Clarke Colton had helped prove that Randall Bowe had tampered with the evidence, planting her hair and fibers on the weapon. She still could hardly believe it all.

Wondered if she'd always be in shock over it...

"So, who would want Fritz dead?" Clarke asked. "Can you think of anyone who might have something to gain from this?"

"Some woman was paid to say that she'd seen me near my house at the time of the murder, when, in fact, I'd been walking in the park downtown, on my dinner break from work. Maybe she has something to do with all of this," she suggested.

He shook his head. "She's already been questioned extensively. She doesn't even know who, ultimately, paid to have her testify. She was approached, needed the money and didn't ask questions..."

Everleigh wondered how little it had taken for the woman to ruin an innocent person's life. A hundred dollars? Two?

And she wondered what might have happened to the woman, to get her to sell her soul in such a way. Nothing good, she was sure.

Life was a lot harder on some than others. Having grown up in the neighborhood she had, she knew that firsthand. Desperation drove people to do unsavory things. She'd seen it again and again in her own volunteer work.

And thanked God every day that she'd been spared. Glancing out his office window, directly beneath the room she'd been allotted, looking out over downtown Grave Gulch, she tried to focus without undue emotion attached to her thoughts. Her memories.

At the time of the murder, she'd been pretty much in shock, dealing with the divorce, and with the fact that Fritz had been spreading rumors about her moral character, labeling her a cheater. And then she'd been arrested. It was just so hard to comprehend it all... and to do so without a feeling of helplessness that...

Wait.

"Fritz lied about me, blaming me for infidelities that didn't happen... What if he did the same to someone else? What if one of his girlfriends was putting pressure on him to leave me, maybe threatening to tell me or someone else about their affair, and he started telling lies about her to protect his reputation?"

It made sense.

Good sense.

And was exactly the kind of thinking she needed to be doing to help herself…

Clarke sat forward, a look of interest on his suddenly businesslike face. "That would establish a motive, for sure," he said, and then turned back to the desktop computer, typing and reading. She was left wondering if she should clear out, head back up to the room that was a much nicer cell than the one she'd left, but pretty much still a cell.

She'd packed in such a hurry, she hadn't brought much with her to do, but she loved to read. And could possibly lose herself in one of the books in her room.

Or she could think about her future. What she wanted to do with it—if she lived to get to it. She needed to find a financial adviser she could trust to help her deal with Fritz's insurance money. And with the sale of the building.

And to call someone to clean up the mess in her house after the crime scene was released. She needed to go through things and get rid of a lot of it. Everything of Fritz's, or anything that reminded her of him, had to go. To his parents. And to the community center…

"There's nothing in here about any of the girlfriends in particular." Clarke's words carried on as though there hadn't been a few minutes' lapse in their conversation.

"I didn't know about them," she told him. "Neither did his family. It stands to reason that he was good at keeping them a secret. Out-of-town weekends tend to help with that." She hadn't meant to be snarky.

This man was helping her. Not holding her hostage.

He wasn't making a prisoner out of her. Her own life choices had done that.

Because she'd been charmed by a charmer.

And now she was sitting across from another one. Her stomach jolted when he turned his compassionate blue eyes on her.

"Word is that you've had a lot of girlfriends," she said. "The guard who was talking to me while we waited for my ride home from prison mentioned it when she told me that it was you who found the evidence that got me exonerated..."

Skin turning red, she knew she couldn't leave it at that. "Because I'd asked her," she admitted, rather than lay the impropriety solely on the guard who'd been only too willing to dish on a Colton. Even though Everleigh knew it was inappropriate, she was genuinely curious.

"You asked her about the number of girlfriends I've had?" He sounded...surprised...but not affronted. More...curious, at least.

"No. Of course not. I asked her where you fell in the family tree. I'd never heard of you until I saw you in court. I knew of Chief Melissa Colton, of course, and Detective Troy Colton, who's your cousin...and that you have other cousins who work in the GGPD..."

"I'm the oldest of four siblings. Three boys and a girl. Melissa is the only one of us who actually works for the GGPD. Travis is the founder and CEO of Colton Plastics, and Stanton is a bodyguard. Dad's Frank Colton, a shipping executive and a really nice guy, by the way, and Mom's the artist he fell in love with while he was on vacation in Italy. I have a number of Colton cousins, many of whom work at the GGPD. And I don't see how any of this leads to conversations about my love life."

He wasn't going to let it go.

She didn't blame him. She'd been out of line, bringing it up.

"I… Just so you know…I don't blame your family for what happened. They were just doing their jobs…"

"Not well enough, if no one had noticed the discrepancies in detective reports and the information coming from forensics," he said. "And I still don't see what any of it has to do with who I've dated…"

"I only asked the guard if you were married. And I asked if Melissa was, too, and Troy. Trying to get a feel for what I was up against in terms of understanding how a spouse would lie about another spouse's infidelity. The guard took it from there." She hadn't been sure if the woman had been trying to warn her off getting any ideas about Clarke Colton—not that Everleigh had been at all interested—or if she had merely been engaging in a bit of gossip.

His expression changed, the interest diminishing a bit…which was fine by her.

But.

She was staying at his house. Was probably going to be in his company, almost exclusively, until they caught whoever had tried to kill her. She had to know who and what he was. Who and what she had to guard against.

She'd fallen for a charmer once. She was apparently susceptible to them. And had to fight off any danger in that area before it had a chance to infiltrate her system.

"I can't help it if women are drawn to me," he said, pulling a little notepad from beneath the laptop and grabbing a pen, as though the subject was done.

"You can help how you react around them," she said. "You don't have to flirt with them just because they're there."

He frowned. "I don't flirt with anyone if they're not receptive to it. And this isn't really any of your business, by the way."

"At least answer me this, since I'm staying here… Is there anyone who's going to take exception to me being here? I don't need any more enemies right now."

"No. And I don't have a girlfriend." His tone had an edge to it. "Now, do you have any idea who any of the women were with whom your husband was having affairs? I think we need to start with them."

Yeah, she thought so, too. And… "I feel so stupid, but no, I truly have no idea. I was still reeling from the fact that he'd seen an attorney and was complaining about the paperwork involved in filing for divorce to even think about putting names to the nebulous factors out there. Maybe one of his girlfriends wasn't happy with the fact that he hadn't officially filed the papers yet. If he'd told her he was dumping me for her…" She'd seen it happen that way on television. Had read about it in books.

Clarke wrote in his notebook. No longer frowning, but his expression was not really friendly anymore, either. Which was just fine. She *had* been prying into his personal life, after all. And couldn't deny she was interested in his answer, despite herself.

"I hate all of this…hate that for the past three months

it's all I can think about…and I still don't have the answers. I wish to God I'd gotten a better look at who tried to run me down this morning, but with that ski mask and the gloves and coat…"

It was like she was being made helpless at every turn, and she'd never been a helpless woman. She was the one who helped others. *Always.*

"I just don't get why, if this is an ex-lover, someone who felt he'd jilted her, she would be looking for something at your house?"

"I don't know." Everleigh shook her head. "I've been trying to figure that out myself. What anyone could have been looking for. But then, Fritz was apparently able to keep a multitude of secrets from me, so what do I really know? It's anybody's guess…"

"If it's okay with you, I plan to ask around about who Fritz has been seen with. And to follow credit-card receipts for out-of-town trips to see if we can pinpoint who he was with."

He looked over at her, his gaze humanizing again, as though he saw her as an individual, not a job, and she was glad. Whether she liked it or not, she was.

She gave him permission to do whatever he needed to do to keep her safe. And hoped to God that the only safety in jeopardy was physical. Because she wasn't at all confident that when it came to her emotional safety, Clarke Colton was the man for the job.

Chapter 5

Everleigh was just getting up to leave Clarke's office when her phone rang. The sound drew his attention to her just in time for him to notice the mixed expression that crossed her face. Dread. But not fear. Resignation. She caught him watching her and his gaze dropped immediately.

Landing on the lovely curves of breasts completely filling out the black sweater she'd had on under her coat. With the tight-fitting jeans and black boots, that tousled blond hair, this woman could have walked out of any fancy lunch place where people went to see and be seen.

And yet…there was nothing flashy about her. The snow on the ground required boots, and jeans and a sweater were pretty much the go-to for winters in their small Michigan town. Not everyone filled out a sweater as she did, however…

The fourth ring had him meeting her gaze again with a sense of his own resignation. She'd caught him staring at her breasts. Best just to own it. So, he did. By holding her gaze openly. Not saying anything. No excuses. Or awkward explanations. Her breasts had captivated his attention for a moment, and now he was looking her in the eye.

"It's my mother," she said.

Taking him out of his own sordid world with a shot back to reality.

"What do I tell them?"

They needed to talk about that.

"Can you call her back?"

She nodded, watching the phone until it stopped ringing.

"Obviously, you have to tell your family you aren't home," Clarke said, back in business mode, with a swear to himself that he wouldn't stray again. "What you tell them as to why is up to you. But you shouldn't tell anyone where you're staying. Not until we know who's after you."

"You think it's a member of my own family?"

"No." He shook his head, but not emphatically. He'd seen stranger things than relatives after each other. "But it could be someone you all know. Someone Fritz knew better than you were aware he did." He shrugged, not wanting to hurt her any more than she'd been already but knowing that he wasn't there to protect her emotional health. He was there to rid her of the threat to her physical safety. "The fact that someone is after you, right after you are exonerated of your husband's murder, and is going through your home… This tells me it's personal. Which means, most likely, the perp is someone you know." He couldn't emphasize the "knowing" part enough. If she underestimated… trusted where she shouldn't…

"How do I know you aren't just isolating me here for some nefarious reason of your own? Taking advantage of what happened this morning?" The question didn't hold a lot of fear, or even a totally serious note in her voice, but he saw the doubt lingering in her gaze.

He handed her his phone. "Find my sister's contact. It's under 'Melissa Colton,'" he said, completely serious, and when she hesitated, he nodded toward the phone without breaking eye contact with her. "Please. I should have done this already. Because you're absolutely right to question me and I'm not going to be able to keep you safe if you don't trust me."

She touched his phone screen. No way he should have been aroused by her slender, gentle fingers on his phone, and it wasn't like he was getting hard or anything, but…jeez. What in the hell was the matter with him? Being attracted to a woman was one thing… Getting all het up about keeping her safe, feeling all überprotective…

"Okay, so your sister's contact information is on your phone," she said.

"Call her."

"I'm not calling the chief of police."

"Call her. She'll understand. That's her personal number. She'll see my name come up. She'll answer." Older brothers had some perks after all, even when they'd spent years bucking the system little sisters stood for.

He watched while she dialed, got a little distracted when the glass that had so recently pressed to his face pressed to hers, and then listened as, with apparently no trepidation at all, she said, "Chief Colton? This is Everleigh Emerson. We met the other day outside the prison..."

A pause followed. His sister would be putting her at ease, letting her know that she remembered her, or some other such thing meant to reassure her. Melissa was a great cop. But she also knew how to deal with people a whole lot better than he did.

Mostly because she had more patience than he did.

He didn't stay in relationships long enough to grow any patience, and after the last debacle...he'd lost a lot of confidence in his ability to set any woman at ease.

"Yes, ma'am. He told me to call, actually, so that..."

Then, "Yeah." The last was accompanied by a somewhat knowing smile, though Everleigh wasn't looking in his direction. And Clarke reassessed the wisdom in his choice to sic his sister on a woman he suddenly wanted to think well of him.

Not just a woman he was trying to protect, but one he wanted to impress?

He tapped on his keyboard. Hard. Looked at the screen he'd brought up. Telling himself he was working when, in fact, he wasn't focusing on a single thing the computer was showing him.

"I will. And...thank you..."

He continued to stare at the screen.

"She said she asked you to keep me safe." He glanced

over to take the phone from her. Had himself back under control. Or more so, anyway.

It wasn't like he was getting all randy and ready to jump her bones, in any event. Noticing beautiful women was just part of being him. Had been since he'd hit puberty. Flirting with them came naturally, too.

Taking it any further than that… He'd never had a complaint in that area. Never pushed himself on a woman, or even came on to one who hadn't already indicated that she'd be open to his advance.

Finding Everleigh Emerson attractive was a nuisance, but not the end of the world. It didn't even mean the end of his ability to do a great job for her without putting her in any kind of a compromising situation.

What was just…unnerving…was the protective instincts the woman was raising in him. He'd had protection jobs before. He'd never felt so…personally invested as he did with this one.

He wanted to ask what else his sister had said, but she had her phone to her ear, saving him from making that mistake into an inappropriate personal foray. "My mom left a voice mail," she said, standing there in front of his desk, owning the room, as far as he was concerned.

When he saw her expression falter, her features falling into a state of nothingness, everything about and within him sharpened. She'd barely ended the call before he asked, "What's wrong?"

Falling back into the chair she'd vacated, she said, "My mom's throwing a big party for me tomorrow night," she said, her tone filled with doom and gloom. "She's invited everyone who's ever been close to me…

and everyone who's ever been close to Gram. It's to welcome me, which I could easily miss if it were up to me…" She winced, her voice carrying a note of hurt, but before he could commiserate, let her know he understood how her mother's mistrust must have pained her, she continued with, "But it's also to gather to show support for Gram, kind of in line with the protests… I can't miss that."

He agreed, but not necessarily for the same reasons. "You don't want to go," he said, homed in on what he was gleaning the most.

"Would you? My family, my own parents, yeah, they came to my defense when I was first arrested, but when the evidence showed that I'd killed Fritz, they all believed it. Every single one of them jumped ship, except for Gram. Not one of them was even swayed by Gram's continued and quite vocal belief in me. None of them helped her get anyone to take another look at my case. If they'd gathered together then, perhaps your sister or another detective would have bothered to take a second look at things. Instead, with even my own parents thinking I did it, Gram had to resort to kidnapping to get anyone to take her seriously…"

He'd worked hard to earn back his family's trust after years of putting them on edge by living by his own set of rules—going out most nights and having fun, skating on the edge of the law when solving cases, seeking out dangerous adventures rather than settling down. Only the fact that he'd had a decent code of ethics had prevented him from losing them more completely…

"Still, for Gram, I have to go…"

"You also need to go so that we can see who's there.

In the first place, it seems likely that you know whoever it is who's after you, and so it stands to reason that the person will be there. Or, on the other hand, if someone key is missing, that's who I'll want to look at. So often, though, perpetrators insinuate themselves into crime scenes and situations. They have to see what effect they're having, keep tabs on what everyone is saying and doing."

"But…how am I going to…? I think it's pretty clear by now that I'm not the greatest at choosing who to trust…"

He wanted to point out that she'd trusted him…but she was right… Until he'd had her call Melissa, she'd taken him at his word for every aspect of their plan. Even moving into his home with him without consulting anyone else.

Yes, he was related to law enforcement. And, yes, he was the one responsible for finding the evidence that won her her freedom…but still…he was also a man who hadn't always followed every letter of the law when conducting his investigations. Results mattered most, he found.

And it made him feel…more…like a better man. Pleased that she'd trusted him enough to move into his home. More of a trustworthy individual. More of a decent human being.

Both little pieces of the self-respect he'd been eroding over the years of balking at societal constraints.

"I have a plan," he said, things occurring to him on the fly, but with that sense of rightness he got when he was on track with an investigation. "You're going to need to trust me on it, though."

"Of course. I'm here, aren't I?" Her expression was completely without guile. She saw him as a means to her safety. Not as a single man, despite her probing questions earlier.

The realization left a sting of disappointment in its wake. But he saw the usefulness of her perspective, too.

Especially considering what he was about to propose.

"I'll accompany you to your party, posing as your new boyfriend. We can say we met because I was the one who exonerated you and it went from there." He spoke the words with a slight sense of anticipation, capped with guilt. It was a solid plan. All bodies of law enforcement used undercover ops because they worked. "That way I can move about freely, asking questions, getting to know people, without tipping anyone off to the fact that I'm investigating them. The ruse is believable in that we can say we met during your time in prison, with the crown jewel being the truth that I'm the one who won you your freedom. We can say that we've spent most of the past two days together."

"If we do that, people will figure out that I'm staying with you."

It wasn't ideal. But… "They don't have to know you're here. You could be in a safe house that I have access to. And, just to reassure you, this place has security at the ground floor, no one can get in the building without a pass, and there are monitored security cameras on every elevator, so anyone attempting to get to you would be seen getting up to my door, which is a hell of a lot safer than your place. And you won't ever be here alone. If I have to go out, someone else will come over to guard the door."

He added, "It's important that you don't go to that party alone. And I don't want to miss this golden opportunity to get a look at everyone in your sphere all at once."

She hadn't balked about the boyfriend part yet. He sat ready to defend the cover.

"Okay." She took the wind out of his sails. But she didn't seem happy about the idea.

"What's bothering you?" He'd been ready to go to bat for his plan. He could still do so. He knew it was the right thing to do. Professionally, anyway. His instincts in that arena rarely steered him wrong.

"Fritz claimed that I was unfaithful to him, and now, two days out of prison, which I went into even before his funeral, I'm showing up with a new boyfriend?"

Maybe he hadn't considered every avenue…having missed one he wouldn't have considered even if he'd had a week to work on the plan. Everleigh's sensibilities. Her reputation…

"We can say that I've insisted that you stay someplace safe, and you aren't telling anyone where it is, if they ask, because the GGPD chose the place and asked you not to disclose it."

"And we've just started seeing each other…when you asked me out to celebrate getting out of prison," she said slowly.

"Or you invited me out to dinner as a thank-you for my great sleuthing…"

She gave him a full grin then, for the first time since they'd entered his home.

And Clarke felt his world start to spin on a dangerous axis.

Chapter 6

Everleigh was still sitting in Clarke's office, worrying about the advisability of pretending that he was her boyfriend, even as she acknowledged that his plan was solid, when his phone rang. Troy calling, as it turned out, letting Clarke know that her house was no longer a crime scene.

"He advises that we head back over there, let you get things put away, and thus have a better chance to tell if anything's missing," Clarke told her, standing up and reaching for the coat he'd had on earlier. He'd thrown it over the arm of the couch along the wall, rather than hanging it on the standing rack right by the door.

Something she'd already noted. She liked his laid-back nature, his lack of rigidity—unlike Fritz, who'd been so adamant that all routines were in place for good reason and deviation from them would cause chaos, which led to a less healthy lifestyle.

Ha! Screwing around had obviously been routine for the real Fritz Emerson and had definitely not been good for his health. Assuming that Clarke was right and one of Fritz's mistresses was his murderer.

"He'd like you to get things put back in their normal places, so you'll know if something's been moved, and then the department's going to set up some security cameras inside the house. Ransacking a house because you're angry is one thing, but with you thinking someone's been in and out of your house...we need to have full-time surveillance going. To know what's going on."

"Could be whoever was there was there to kill me and just chickened out." She'd been kind of thinking that all morning.

Until he shook his head. "Doesn't make sense. This is probably the same person who murdered your husband in that same house by bashing his head in with a paperweight. More likely, the perp is looking for something. And if they didn't find it this morning, chances are, they'll be back."

His words made her shiver. Not in a good way.

And she hoped whoever was after something had found it. Or would just ask for it. There was nothing in that house that was worth more to her than her safety and freedom. And she was determined never to lose those again.

Clarke helped where he could at Everleigh's house. Not one to stand around idly, or to be good with little to do, he busied himself with straightening and organizing, so that Everleigh could come behind him and put things away where they belonged. He'd established straight-out with Everleigh that he would stay close to her. The police had just cleared out. He knew there was no one else in the house. But that didn't mean someone couldn't come in. Most particularly since she'd had the feeling someone had been in the house the night before.

Everleigh didn't argue.

They tackled the kitchen first and worked as though they'd been on the job together for years, not like they were inventing it as they went along.

She was completely quiet at first. He left her to her thoughts. Wondered a bit about what kind of memories she'd made in the house. And how much of what she was touching reminded her of her deceased husband.

As she put away the groceries, she offered to make them some grilled ham-and-cheese sandwiches for lunch, then to bring the fruits and vegetables to his place. Since he wasn't good at grocery shopping—he tended to forget about fresh food and let it spoil on his watch—he accepted the offer. But he refused to make anything of the sudden rush of warmth that came at the thought of her being at his place for the next few days.

He'd had houseguests before. Enjoyed having people around.

He didn't ever get warm and gooey about it.

What was it about this ex-prisoner barmaid that was making him feel this way?

Maybe the way she was talking about what they'd have for dinner. She had some chicken enchilada meal she'd been planning to make to freeze in portions for herself. He hadn't planned on having her cook for him. Or care for him.

But seeing the way she seemed to lighten up as she talked about the cooking, he readily agreed. He liked enchiladas. And didn't get home-cooked meals all that often. Still, she was his guest. Partially because the GGPD had screwed up. No way he should be taking advantage…

And then it dawned on him. Cooking would be something she'd have done as a normal part of her day. And normalcy would help her cope.

The thought made him feel less guilty for letting her do such nice things for him.

And the prospect of home-cooked meals could explain his pleasure at the idea of having her around. If he'd only started being drawn to her *after* she'd offered to cook for him…

Moving from the kitchen to the dining and living rooms after lunch, they made good progress, talking a little more. About music choices as he straightened a collection of CDs that rivaled his own. His younger siblings bought all their music digitally and had gotten him more into the habit as well, but he still liked having the physical copies on hand. Liked having control of what he owned.

And liked that Everleigh also had an appreciation for country music. They'd even both been to a couple of the same concerts in Detroit and Ann Arbor in recent years.

Things got a little more complicated when they moved to the back half of the house. Without any conversation at all, he avoided her bedroom, and she tended to it alone, while he cleaned up a rather sizable mess of spilled cleaning product in the hallway bathroom just down from her opened door. It was the only overt damage caused in the entire place. The only place where frustration seemed to have gotten the better of the burglar. Because it was the last room he or she was in?

Or was there another reason the bathroom had set them off? Pulling his notepad out of the back pocket of his jeans, he jotted down the questions.

They met up in what was obviously her office. The decor in the room was decidedly feminine, with floral wall art, angels on shelves that hadn't been touched—another note for his pad.

And masses of piles of books, having been pulled from an entire wall, floor to ceiling, of shelves. His height came in handy there, and as she handed him books, he reorganized them, starting with the top shelf.

Noticing titles, particularly, so that he didn't notice her so close by, bending over, standing up, that body with those lovely curves moving with such grace. And the floral scent… It wasn't strong. Not like some perfumes, which tended to gag him sometimes, but more subtle. A breeze on a summer day that caught a waft of a rose garden…

The thought stopped him cold. And then he double-timed the shelving. When had he ever been aware of a summer breeze before? Had he ever even seen a rose garden?

He'd been handed a couple of self-help books. As though she knew how badly he needed them. Just in case, he read the taglines. And then those on the next books, too. Apparently, there was going to be an entire shelf filled with ways to better yourself. Financially—some books written by names he recognized. Emotionally—he'd never heard of the authors. One book in particular, about being an effective person in all walks of life, he'd actually read himself once.

Probably more recently than she had, judging by the wear and tear on her copy. His was less than five years old. He stood there, looking at the book…and at her, quietly working her way through cleaning up another mess in her life that she hadn't made. She hadn't said much since they'd begun the task of cleaning up. Hadn't cried, either. Or showed other signs of distress.

She'd just gone about the business of quietly cleaning up.

"What?" Books in hand ready to give him, Everleigh stood there, frowning. He shelved the books she'd already handed him. Took the next…

Had no idea how to answer her. He wouldn't lie but his thoughts were definitely not case related.

"You have a problem with self-help books in general or just the effectiveness one?" she asked on the next handoff.

"Are these all yours?" he prevaricated. Not a great response, but the best he could do on the fly. This woman had had him off-kilter since the adrenaline burst with which he'd rescued her that morning and he had to get himself in check.

"Yeah. Fritz's stuff is mostly still here," she said, bending for more books. "He moved out a month before his murder, but he got a furnished place and didn't take much more than clothes and toiletries with him. He still came home to work in his den every day while

I was at the bar." It was the longest conversation she'd offered him since they'd arrived. Because they were almost done? Or was she loosening up some with him around? "But he wasn't much of a reader."

"I can't imagine not reading. All the information out there…" Not to mention the entertainment.

"He said he got the same in podcasts and watching the news…"

He didn't really want to talk about Fritz Emerson—not unless it led him to knowing who wanted him dead.

"And you still didn't answer my question," she said, becoming persistent at the most inopportune time. Books in hand, she didn't give them to him, just stood there looking over at him. "You had a really odd look on your face. You have something against that book? I mean, I've seen your house. Clearly, you're a reader, too. And that book… I pretty much live by it…"

"I like the book."

"You've read it, then?"

"Yeah. It's on the shelf in my office," Clarke admitted.

"So, why the look?"

Why wasn't she giving up?

"Why does it matter?" he asked.

"I don't know, but it does."

Everleigh was reasonable. And apparently when she knew something was going on that concerned her, she could also be obstinate.

"The book…it's practical and full of wisdom for anyone who wants to live their best life…"

He sounded like a…someone who was not him.

"And you have a problem with that?"

"No." Crossing his arms when she still didn't give him books, he raised his chin and gave it to her. "I have a problem with the fact that your book is so much older than my copy. You might have come from what some around here call 'the wrong side of the tracks,' but you didn't let that define you. Instead, you took charge and made more out of your life…"

He was saying it all wrong. He knew it as the words came out.

"And you have a problem with that?" she repeated. Her frown was back.

"Of course not." He bit back more words. "The opposite, in fact. You probably have an older copy because you used the book and its advice to help make a better life for yourself. In contrast, I had a lot of opportunity, and instead of being grateful and taking advantage of that, I squandered away the first ten years of my adulthood and spent the next five earning back the respect I'd lost in the process. I've got the book. But I only read it for the first time four and a half years ago."

As the words escaped him, giving her more than he ever gave anyone, her expression changed. She was still assessing him, but with more curiosity and respect than the earlier frown had portrayed.

The frown probably had been better for his libido. And for their current situation. He needed her to trust him to keep her safe. And to pretend to like him when they went to her mother's the next night.

Not to respect or actually like him…even if he now respected *and* liked her.

* * *

She'd saved Fritz's den for last. Hadn't been in the room for a month before her husband was killed, and hadn't been in since, either.

"I have no real idea where things go," she said, scooping stuff up off the floor...papers, an ashtray she didn't recognize, a box of cigars, baseball cards. "This was his space, even when our marriage was... well...a marriage," she amended. At no time had it been healthy.

And how she'd managed to avoid that fact for eighteen years was about to drive her nuts. About as much as the fact that her own parents had thought her capable of murder.

It was like her whole life she'd lived in a little world of her own—until recently. How did she trust herself to know anything now? And if she couldn't trust herself, how did she trust anyone else?

The only trustworthy person had been Gram, apparently. At least, it seemed that way to Everleigh, as she tried to get the room in shape as quickly as possible so they could get out of there.

The silence started to overwhelm her...the deafening white noise inside turning her inner thoughts into a loudspeaker.

"The more I think about it, the more I realize that Fritz and I had been living separate lives for most of our marriage," she said aloud, caring more about getting out of her internal hell than exposing herself to Clarke Colton. It wasn't like this PI was a part of her life, like she'd ever see him again once whoever had tried to kill her was caught.

"It kind of seems that way," he said, his tone agreeable. Nonjudgmental. "You said he didn't move much out of the house, but pretty much every room, they all have your touch. Except here."

Straightening, she turned to look at him righting Fritz's basketball memorabilia on the shelves allotted to it.

"How do you know what's my touch and what's his?" she asked, curious. And kind of wanting him to be right, too.

"This room is nothing like the rest of the house. And you just told me it was mostly Fritz's room."

The answer was so simple. And yet…right, too.

Right under her nose.

Like her failing marriage had been? She and Fritz hadn't been as close, but she'd told herself marriages had ups and downs. And maybe she'd buried herself in charity work so she didn't have to see just how far apart they'd grown.

"My guess is that's why you didn't know about the cheating," he continued in the same conversational tone. Hitting a chord deep within her. Batting at the doubts trying to suffocate her ability to think straight. "Because you were living separate lives."

She stared at him. He'd just been making conversation, but could he be right?

She wanted him to be right. Sort of. Needed the explanation he was handing her.

And yet…why had she stayed?

"I wanted kids," she said, stuffing fishing tackle back in boxes. "He said he did, too. We tried for years and he seemed as disappointed as I was that we weren't having any, but kept putting off going for testing, and yet kept saying we should go together. Didn't do me much good to find out it wasn't me, if we didn't know it was him. And if it was me…maybe I didn't want to know that, either."

Why in the hell was she bringing that up? Except that…she'd asked the question. Silently, yeah, but…

Some things had been in there too long. Her life was unraveling faster than she could hold on to it and she had to find a way to make sense of enough of it to move forward. To give herself a future.

"I found out six years ago that he'd had a vasectomy shortly after we were married…"

She should have left then.

And still, she'd stayed. She'd made her choice. Vowed to be faithful to it. And that had meant something to her.

Far more than it had meant to him, obviously.

But she hadn't known that.

She'd really thought that Fritz loved her. And had been petrified of being a father.

Maybe he had loved her, in his own way. Maybe she just hadn't loved herself enough to demand more for herself. Maybe she'd thought she deserved to have to settle?

She didn't know. Was tired of asking.

But knew she couldn't stop. The only way to move forward was to learn from her mistakes. And yet, looking at herself from his eyes—from the eyes of someone only just meeting her, someone who was gaining instant access into the intimate details of her life—she felt like such a failure.

When he'd held that book and told her that she'd

made more of her opportunities than he had… Did he really see her that way?

Or was he just being kind? She'd learned long ago that if something looked too good to be true, it probably was. And because of her choices, her eighty-year-old gram was sitting in prison…

"Hey, come on…" An arm suddenly wrapped around her shoulders. She hadn't even known Clarke had approached, had barely felt him drop to the hardwood floor beside her. "You're doing great," he told her. "Just a little bit more and we can get out of here."

She didn't really want to get out of there. "There" was her home. Her haven.

What she wanted was to get Fritz out of there once and for all. To take back what was hers. And to make it better.

She wanted to love and be loved.

To be worthy of the kind of emotion she had to give.

She'd wanted to be a mother. A partner. A homemaker. And a salon owner, too.

So how had she ended up with none of those things? She had to figure it out. Quick.

And the first step was to quit burying her head in the sand. Or just looking at the moment in front of her. That got her through days. It had gotten her through two months in prison and an agonizing trial. It was time to do more than just get through. Time to ask what she wanted.

Time to… Clarke didn't speak, just sat there, his arm supporting her back, his hand at her shoulder. A Colton. Sitting on the floor holding her up as though she was some kind of fine china.

She'd never been breakable. But she'd once thought herself delicate.

And worthy of being handled that way. Hadn't even noticed her self-confidence shedding away.

How was it that turning to look at Clarke Colton just then made her feel like she was getting some of it back?

"Why would he do that?" she whispered, their mouths only inches apart. "Why would he say he wanted kids and then have surgery so he couldn't? And not tell me? Why take away my chances to have a family of my own?"

"My guess is because he didn't want to lose you. Or share you."

She watched his lips move. Felt the heat of his body as he held her against him. She didn't lean into that embrace, but she absorbed it.

"Then why cheat on me all these years? If I wasn't enough to…"

His finger touched her lips. "Shhh. Don't say it, and as much as you can help it, don't even think it."

His blue eyes were pools of compassion, of assurance, and she didn't have the strength to pull her own gaze away from them. She wallowed there, searching him. Letting him see her.

"The man was a fool…" His words were as soft as hers had been as his mouth lowered and…touched hers. Lightly. Gently.

Oh, so sweetly.

Everleigh sat there, her face raised to his, letting him move his mouth on hers. She didn't respond. Just let the shock of it all consume her. But when he went to pull away, she groaned and reached her face up to him, her hands flat on the floor, bracing her, while she kissed him back.

Chapter 7

What in the hell was he doing?

Even as Clarke leaned into the kiss, he started to pull back. Had to stop what was starting…to make it go away, not just in the moment, but permanently.

He was on the job. Would absolutely not sacrifice the hard years he'd spent earning back the trust of his family or his professional reputation. He was done jumping into what felt good in the moment.

And more…he couldn't take advantage of Everleigh Emerson when she was vulnerable. She deserved so much better.

His lips still moving against hers, his body aching to press against hers, he tore his mouth away, wiped it with the back of his wrist as he stood up.

Scrambling for a way to stay on the job so that he could keep her safe.

A way to maintain her trust in light of what had just happened. A way to ensure that it didn't happen again.

"I'm sorry," he said. "I…have never…in my entire career…made a move on a client." He was breathing hard still. His words were punctuated by the deep breaths; he needed to figure out what he was doing.

She nodded. Busied herself finishing up with the fishing tackle. Not looking at him.

And he realized…she'd kissed him back. As opposed to pushing him away.

Did she *want* him to kiss her again?

Was she hurt by his rejection? That idea was alarming.

He stood there watching her filling sections of the plastic container with hooks and flies and lures with no rhyme or reason to their organization. Her fingers… so slim and gentle compared to his own…

He couldn't have sex with her. And the temptation would be that much more dangerous if he thought she wanted him to.

He didn't want to hurt her. In the short or long term.

He absolutely didn't want to start any kind of relationship, either. With anyone… The last burn was still stinging with a little too much repulsion for him to even open that door.

"You asked if I have a current girlfriend…" The words started to roll, and while he wasn't sure of them, he didn't stop them. "I don't, but I did. Aubrey agreed that we were only having fun, enjoying each other's company, but she read far more into things than was there. To the point that I was uncomfortable. She started checking up on me, didn't want me going anywhere without her, and when I ended things, she wouldn't go away. Kept calling in tears, texting. Driving by. Trying to talk to my family. When all of that got her nowhere, she threatened some things…"

He sounded like some kind of victim of an abusive relationship. That hadn't been the message he'd wanted to impart. Everleigh didn't look at him, but her fingers on the tackle had slowed. And when she turned, her eyes glaring points at him, he knew he should have kept his mouth shut.

"You think I'm going to make something out of one kiss?" she asked. "Or that I'd resort to running to Melissa, tattling on you?"

He couldn't tell if she was more hurt or pissed… "No!" He advanced, but at her steely look, he backed up again. "That wasn't where I was going. At all," he said, putting all of the conviction inside him in his voice. In the look he gave her. "I swear. I just… I like women, Everleigh. I've known a lot of them. I'm forty years old," he added, as though the "a lot of women" needed justification. "But that's all it is. Liking them, and if they like me back, we see if there's something between us. I enjoy lighthearted relationships that aren't going anywhere…"

He sounded so shallow. And it wasn't that, either. He just…

Didn't know what it was.

He'd started the conversation to distract her from what appeared to be a mutual attraction. Maybe to show her that he was the type of man she'd never want. Someone like her husband—minus the cheating—

even if he knew he was entirely different from Fritz Emerson.

But all he'd done was confuse himself.

"I find you…intriguing," he said. "And I feel for you…your situation. Seeing you sit there…sorting tackle, cleaning up your ransacked house without a single complaint…having just been released from prison after being there for something you didn't do…"

She closed the tackle box. Stood up, put it in a cupboard with the rest of the boxes and shut the door. Then turned to him.

"You're saying you kissed me out of pity?"

No, it hadn't been that, either.

"I'm saying…it should never have happened. It was unprofessional, and though I find you attractive, I don't know why I overstepped. It wasn't anything I've ever done before, and I am absolutely certain it shouldn't ever happen again."

She nodded, her expression placid. Opened her mouth, but before she got a word out, a sound came from the direction of the kitchen. Like a door handle rattling.

Clarke was out of the room and to the back of the house before he'd taken a breath.

Only to see the main door leading to the backyard closed and locked, and the screen door behind it hanging open. He ran out into the yard, saw the back gate open, with no one in sight.

By the time Clarke made it back into the house, Everleigh had herself firmly in hand. Yeah, some bad things had happened to her. But she was still there. Still okay.

And needed herself to be strong. To take control and deal with the circumstances she'd been dealt.

Not be some guy's pity kiss.

Someone was clearly after her, after something in her house.

"What person in their right mind vandalizes a house, tries to run someone down and then comes back to the same house hours after the police have been through it?" she asked, as she rode with Clarke back to his condo. Along with the food, she'd brought her tablet and charger, too, so she could stream shows in her room and still have her phone free. Yeah, she was kind of on lockdown again, but Clarke's house was nothing like prison.

She was free to do what she wanted when she wanted.

And she was free to leave, too, if she chose to do so.

"I'd say that person probably isn't in their right mind," Clarke said, glancing at her and then back at the road. "Which is what makes them so dangerous. We can't predict what they might do. Or rest assured that normal protection protocols will work. We need to keep you inside and be on guard at all times." How he made such alarming news sound reassuring, she didn't know.

But the man made her feel safe. In a world that hadn't felt that way for a long, long time.

Which was no reason to kiss him back.

Pity kiss. She admitted to herself that she wanted

to believe that was what it had been because that interpretation simplified everything.

He'd behaved with perfect decorum since reentering her home and saying they had to leave twenty minutes before. Had waited silently for her to collect what she needed and helped carry everything out to the car.

It was as though those out-of-this-world seconds followed by awkward moments in Fritz's den had never happened.

That was exactly what her response to his kiss had been. The first time in more than eighteen years her lips had joined with a man's who wasn't her husband…

Ironic that it had happened in the cheater's den.

Kind of icky that it had also been the room in which her husband had been murdered.

Such was her life.

Feeling like a sitting duck, as she rode beside him with glass from the car windows surrounding them, she watched his hands on the wheel, thinking about what he'd said earlier.

That was better than worrying about a bullet aimed at her shattering the glass.

He found her intriguing.

She didn't hate that.

But there'd be no more kisses between them.

She'd already known he was a womanizer. And while he hadn't confirmed the rumor when she'd brought it up that morning, she knew it was no mistake that he'd done so that afternoon. He was letting her know that he was not relationship material.

His honesty endeared him to her.

But she'd do well to heed his warning, as well. If

she'd had any doubts about the inadvisability of letting that kiss happen a second time, he'd laid them firmly to rest.

She'd never intended to let anything happen between them, in any case. While she didn't blame the Coltons for what had happened to her, she didn't want anyone associated with law enforcement in her sphere. She just wanted to put the whole thing behind her.

Just had one point of curiosity…

"What ended up happening to her? The woman who was stalking you?" The man was related to pretty much the entire GGPD.

"She wasn't stalking me."

Interesting take on it. "What would you call it?"

"Having a hard time taking no for an answer."

Yeah, and she hadn't been a victim of a near murder that morning, either, because who, after all, wanted to be that?

"So, what happened to her?" she asked.

Gram had always said that if you wanted to get out of your own misery, think of someone else's. The advice had worked in prison.

"She ended up getting some professional help and last I knew was living upstate with a relative."

The way he said it…*ended up getting professional help…*

She studied him as he drove, noticing how, once again, his gaze seemed to be on the road, and all around them, too. Like he'd be able to dodge a bullet if it came at them?

"That was it? She just decided she needed help?"

she prodded him, wondering how he had handled being a target—like she'd been.

"In exchange for not having charges pressed against her."

Wow. So, it *had* been big. Couldn't have been easy for him to deal with. And yet he wore it well. Hadn't seemed to have shaken his peace of mind—at least, from what little she knew of him thus far.

She wanted that. To be able to take the things that happened to her and continue forward, having learned from them, but not letting them stop her from moving on to what was next.

As he drove, keeping his lookout, she just had to say, "Thank you."

"For what?" His glance was lingering, but his attention turned immediately back to the road, reminding her that there could be danger all around her.

"Your honesty." She told him the truth, and then, feeling awkward, she added, "And everything."

When he shot her a glance, looking like he had something to say, but not saying it, she said, "I find you intriguing, too, but I have no intention of that kiss ever happening again." He just drove. "And no desire, whatsoever, to become involved with a PI who works with the GGPD."

Now, that was too harsh. "Or anyone. Not yet. Not for a long while." Her heart reached out to him. Feeling what he must have gone through, having a woman he'd been intimately involved with try to threaten him.

At least with Fritz, it had all just been him being a creep. A liar. All things the mind had a place for…

But Clarke…there he was…coming off one bad relationship and kissing an ex-con barmaid client.

She wanted to reassure him…she wasn't as bad off as she came across…

"It was the first time I've kissed a man other than Fritz since he and I first started dating…"

She didn't go around just getting physical with other men. Not even after her husband had left her. His lies about her cheating had prevented her from even thinking about doing that—until now.

Which, knowing Fritz and his manipulative ways, had probably been a secondary intention when he'd concocted the lies to begin with. Protect his own reputation with his family, first, and control her, second.

"He wanted me," she said aloud. "He just didn't want to be *faithful* to me. Or want me to be my own person, either." She'd had goals, dreams of her own. He hadn't wanted that, so he'd made sure, behind her back, that it didn't happen.

She looked up at Clarke. "That's the first time I've fully realized that," she told him. "I was like a possession. Not a real person to him…"

And all the while, she'd been committed to making their vows matter, to being true and loyal, to making the marriage work, rather than walking out on it when times got tough.

"What an idiot I was."

"No!" His shoulders, even bigger in the confined space due to the heavy coat he wore, seemed to loom so large. The car's heater was on, but the late afternoon chill still filled the air. "Don't judge yourself by his failings," he told her.

"I chose him."

"You chose what he presented himself to be. The lies are on him."

She'd buy that, except… "How do I know, how does anyone ever know, what's really inside someone else's head?" she asked him. "I fell for Fritz's lies. What's to say I wouldn't fall for another guy like that? I should have been able to sense that something was off…"

"Except that it probably wasn't off at first. Or maybe wasn't ever all the way off. I'm guessing there was a part of him that was the man you saw, the man you loved. Part of him who wanted to be that man."

"Maybe." Or maybe Clarke was just being kind. "But the cheating… They say a woman knows. I didn't."

"Sometimes we only see what we expect to see."

She frowned. "You think I didn't want to know he was cheating, so I subconsciously turned a blind eye to it, mentally as well as physically?"

"I'm saying that you believed him to be one thing and so that was what you saw. You had faith in your husband, Everleigh. That's a good thing."

So why didn't it *feel* good? Why did it leave her alone at thirty-eight with no family of her own, no kids, no career and feeling like a fool…and having to hide out in a gorgeous man's luxury condominium and pretend he was her boyfriend, just to try to save her life?

Ping! A sound came from just behind her, down by the seat. Jerking with a force that slammed her hand into the door handle, she ducked just as Clarke said "Get down!" with enough urgency to fill her with fear.

The car sped up so fast the force sent her backward into the seat. Then he swerved, and her shoulder hit the console beside her. She hid, fear consuming her, and waited for Clarke to give the all clear.

"It's safe now," he said thirty seconds later. She sat up, glancing at the inside of the secure parking garage underneath his condominium building.

"What was that?" she asked, but she knew, her heart beating so loud she could count the beats.

"Sounded like a gunshot to me," he said, looking in the rearview mirror, and off to both sides of them as he pulled out his phone. They were not only underground, but the entry was secured by a guard in a booth, with car admittance only possible with a windshield transmitter that opened the gate. There were security cameras. They'd be checked.

And a little while later, a police officer, standing outside her car door, confirmed that a bullet had hit Clarke's vehicle just behind and below the window where Everleigh's head had been.

Gathering her things, she got out of the SUV, trying not to notice Clarke's solid warmth beside her, or his body practically wrapping around hers as he guided her toward the very private, very quiet elevator up to his home.

She was shaking. Needing a feel-good to get her out of the hell her life had become. And still trying not to remember that she was intrigued by her protector.

That he'd been breathing heavy after he'd kissed her...

Because she was completely serious about not letting him touch her again in that way. About not responding to him. No matter how attractive she might find him.

Or how safe he made her feel.

Chapter 8

The night was easier to get through than he'd supposed. Everleigh made the enchiladas, as she'd said she'd do, while he worked in his office, getting reports from officers in the field around Fritz Emerson's health spa, and from his family at police headquarters, too. So far, no one was talking about any woman Fritz might have been sleeping with. And there'd been no prints, other than Everleigh's and Fritz's, found in the Emerson home. Whoever had broken into Everleigh's home had worn gloves. There'd been no sign of a shooter, or any shell casings, in the block between the latest attempt on Everleigh's life and his home, either.

He hadn't noticed any vehicles following them. Or any suspicious behavior. The security cameras hadn't caught anything and the police investigation didn't turn up anything, either.

Which meant that whoever was after Everleigh was either damn lucky, or someone who fit so completely into the world around them that Clarke and Everleigh could be looking straight at the criminal and not seeing them acting oddly in any way.

That strengthened his theory that the perp might be one of Fritz's secret past mistresses, someone who didn't stand out in any way. Nothing else made sense. The Emersons hadn't been in any substantial debt. There'd been no gambling or failed business ventures, other than the health club that was no longer supporting itself but had been solely owned by Fritz.

They'd found a vehicle that matched the description of the car that had almost run Everleigh down that morning. It was dumped in a ditch not far from the grocery store, on a road that was no more than a long stretch of trees, so there were no cameras anywhere to show who got out of the vehicle. The cops told him that the car had been reported stolen that morning.

And the security cameras in the junkyard where it'd been stolen weren't working.

When he went out to the kitchen to fill Everleigh in on the developments, he found a space empty of human occupation, with a note on the countertop telling him for how long and at what temperature to heat up his dinner. She'd gone to her room for the night.

Obviously expecting to be left alone. Her message couldn't have been any clearer.

When he'd headed up to bed, hours after consuming two helpings of enchiladas, he'd seen her light on under her door. Had knocked and at the same time called out, asking if she was okay or needed anything.

She'd responded immediately, telling him she was fine.

And that was good-night.

She'd managed to defuse their…momentarily off course…situation all on her own. He was grateful to her. Really.

But he went to sleep and dreamed about being her boyfriend.

Everleigh called the prison to check on her grandmother before she'd even showered the next morning. She'd done the same each day since her own release.

Gram was fine, slept well, was eating enough, according to the guard who'd agreed to give her updates.

Everleigh hadn't slept worth a darn, though. The strange bed…down the hall from a man she couldn't get out of her mind.

For most all of her adult life she'd been tied to Fritz. Monogamous. Loyal to the vows she'd taken. Maybe her bizarrely strong awareness of Clarke Colton was just because he was the first man with whom she'd been in extensive contact since her husband's death.

Or maybe her attraction to Clarke was just adrenaline overload, she decided as, naked in the shower, she could hardly touch her breasts or spend much time cleaning her other private parts without igniting the fire that seemed to be tingling there almost nonstop.

She hadn't been that sensitive even in the first months of having sex with Fritz, and she'd thought *that* had been pretty amazing.

Someone still wanted her dead and was getting bolder…

Yeah, it was the fear, being shot at and almost run

over…being framed for murder and sitting in a cell for two months. Gratitude to the man who'd proved her not guilty.

And living in the same space as him. Sharing accommodations and food.

Needing to rely on him for her physical safety.

But what about his scheme, pretending that he was her boyfriend? As she looked over the few outfits she'd brought, she thought about the party they'd be attending together that night—as boyfriend and girlfriend. She wanted to look her best. Wanted to show all the disbelievers that she'd not only survived prison, she was just fine without their support or belief in her.

Still, her stomach knotted with nerves every time she thought about the evening ahead. How did she pretend that the gorgeous, intense, protective Clarke Colton was involved with her, and not start to wish it was true? Or worse, start to get turned on by him? How did she hang on his arm and get turned *off*?

And how did she go there and not hang on to the support he was offering while she faced all of the people she'd loved all her life, knowing that they hadn't known her, or believed in her, at all? What if it was one of them who had killed Fritz for some reason and might actually want her dead?

The knots turned to butterflies and she grabbed her newest pair of skinny stretch jeans, the name-brand pair, and the black sweater she'd paid too much for the week after Fritz had left her. Its softness was what had first drawn her to it, but the way it fit her breasts, slimming at the waist and hugging her just above the hips... Yeah, she needed that extra little boost of confidence.

The black boots were new, too, purchased from one night's worth of tips also during that first week after Fritz left. That purchase had been on the day she'd found out that he'd been cheating on her for years. Her friend Larissa, another waitress at Howlin' Eddie's, had told her the way the boots zipped just to her ankles made her calves look sexy.

And she'd been feeling anything but recently.

Larissa had been there for her a lot during those horrible days of facing the truth about her marriage. They'd spent more than one night on the couch with glasses of wine, talking long into the night.

And Larissa was the one person who'd never vocally said that, once she'd seen the facts, she believed Everleigh killed Fritz. She'd never said she didn't believe it. She hadn't sided with Gram. Hadn't come out and stated that there was no way Everleigh could have done it. But she hadn't sided with the rest of those who'd known her her whole life, either. And that counted for something in Everleigh's book.

Thankfully, Everleigh's mother hadn't invited Janet or any of the other waitresses from the bar, but Larissa was supposed to be at the party that night, too. She was the one sort of bright spot as Everleigh thought of the night ahead. Except that she dreaded the big deal Larissa would make of Everleigh having a new hunky boyfriend. A Colton, no less.

When she'd put off going downstairs as long as she thought she could without looking like she was a little mouse afraid to venture out, Everleigh unlocked her bedroom door and took the staircase as though she owned it. Her makeup was perfect. She'd put earrings in both piercings. And her sassy hair gave her an edge over the nearly scared-witless woman lurking inside her.

For all that, Clarke wasn't in the kitchen. Or the living room she had to pass through to get there. For all she knew, he slept in late. When pictures of that muscled body lying naked on top of the sheets came to mind, she shook her head and made for the coffee maker she'd seen at the end of the counter when she'd been cooking the night before.

It already had coffee in the pot. She poured a cup, figuring she could head back upstairs for a bit, hadn't even had the first sip when Clarke came out of the room off the far end of the living room and into the kitchen.

He was in jeans again, too, and the light brown sweater, along with a pair of brown work shoes that looked waterproofed against the snow, gave him a ruggedness her libido didn't need. He was a definite case of imagination overload.

He didn't ask how she'd slept. Or thank her for dinner, either, though she'd already peeked in the refrigerator to see that the dish she'd left for him was gone. Instead, he began to list all the evidence that her case was lacking.

Which all pretty much led to no leads. Anyplace. Broken cameras, no cameras, neighbors seeing nothing… abandoned car, no shell casings, no fingerprints… It was like a phantom was after her.

She'd almost think she was imagining things if

Clarke hadn't witnessed both attempts on her life. Before helplessness could completely overwhelm her, he continued with his report.

"I'm on my way out..." No. That wasn't a report. Panic flared. He'd said he was going to keep her safe, and in less than twenty-four hours he was walking out on her?

Her mouth fell open... She could only imagine the shock on her face based on his immediate step forward and look of compassion.

"Don't worry," he quickly assured her. "You won't be here alone. And I'll only be gone as long as absolutely necessary..."

Two things registered. He wasn't leaving her alone. And he was coming back.

"I'll be absolutely fine here by myself," she said, finding her groove again. *He's coming back.*

He shook his head. "I'm not taking any chances. And neither is my family."

She liked how he brought the others into the conversation. Into the home, into their fake relationship. And was sure he'd done so on purpose. As a reminder to her.

And to him, too?

He'd been so quick to step forward in her moment of ridiculous panic.

Everleigh could tell that she intrigued him. He'd never kissed a woman on a case before.

God, she was losing her mind. Had Fritz's defection made her so completely starved for male attention that she was glomming on to the first guy in her sphere? Even when her life was in danger?

If she was going to die, she might as well live through a good moment or two first, instead of going out on all the bad ones.

She pushed the wayward thought aside, listening as Clarke said, "My brother Stanton is on his way over now. He's a bodyguard…"

She nodded. "I know who he is," she said. Stanton Colton owned a small but elite protection agency, well-known in town, and his clients were all movie stars and politicians. People with stature and enough money to afford to pay top dollar for their lives. "And there's no way he needs to waste his time on me," she said.

Even with her life-insurance windfall, the idea of paying for even an hour of that kind of protection was bothersome. Wasteful…

"The decision's already been made. He'll be here in less than five minutes, and you won't be paying for any of this—I already told you that. I won't be gone more than an hour or two. And I'm just heading over to the police station."

That got her attention, as he'd probably known it would. "Why?"

"I can't say a lot yet, but Melissa called an emergency meeting for the task force working on the Randall Bowe case…"

"Do they think maybe he has something to do with what's been happening to me since I got out of prison?" As awful as the thought was, she found it more manageable than accepting that someone she knew wanted her dead.

Or that Fritz's killer was after her, too.

Her husband's murderer had been skilled enough to

get away with it, leaving no evidence that led to any solid clues. Did that mean that he'd get Everleigh, too, and no one would ever know why?

"I don't really know for sure what it's about," he said, and she knew he was prevaricating. He'd turned to leave the room but swung around. "I'll ask Melissa how much of it all I can share with you and we'll talk when I get back, okay?"

As though she had any choice… Still, he was being considerate. Nice, even.

She nodded. "And, Clarke?"

He glanced at her, just briefly, but long enough for her to feel the warmth of his gaze.

"Thank you."

He leaned as though he was going to move toward her, but before he'd taken a step, there was a knock at the front door and he was gone.

Clarke was reluctant to leave Everleigh, even just to make a quick trip to the police station. As though no one but him could keep Everleigh safe.

In truth, his brother was more equipped, better trained even than Clarke in terms of guarding actual bodies, but Everleigh felt safe with Clarke. He didn't want to jeopardize that.

The stricken look on her face, when he'd first told her he was leaving…

It took him a second to realize that he'd been speaking to a woman whose husband of eighteen years had just walked out on her a few months before—leaving her understandably sensitive to broken expectations where sticking around was concerned.

Because he'd put off actually leaving his condominium until the last minute—having stood there talking with Stanton, even after the introductions had been made and Everleigh had excused herself to go upstairs to her room—he was the last one to arrive at the emergency meeting.

Melissa was already seated at the head of the table in the small conference room at police headquarters. Two of his cousins, detective Troy and FBI agent Bryce, were already seated on either side of the chief, with two other officers next to them, leaving the other end seat for Clarke. While he could really use a cup of coffee, he refrained from holding them up any longer.

Refrained from doing anything that would require him to be gone from home any longer than absolutely necessary.

"Thanks for coming on such short notice," Melissa said, flipping a strand of red hair over her shoulder. Clarke read the very real concern on his sister's face, but he noticed the new light in those blue eyes, too, and was happy for her. At thirty-six, Melissa had always been single-mindedly devoted to career through and through. And now here she was, in a blink, falling in love with the owner of the hotel where Hannah kidnapped the toddler, and Melissa was already engaged to be married.

And he was absolutely not drawing any ideas for himself from his sister's example, he told himself.

"It looks like we might have another killer on our hands, guys."

Whoa. *What?* Clarke's attention 100 percent on his

sister's words now, he pulled his notebook and pen out of his coat pocket, opened it and started writing.

"Three months ago, Vincent Gully, a man in his fifties, was killed while walking his dog at night in Grave Gulch Park. He was shot point-blank in the chest, cash had been taken from his wallet, and he'd been posed with his hands laid neatly over his abdomen."

Clarke remembered the case. "A suspect was arrested from DNA evidence found at the scene that matched him through the help of a genealogy website," he said.

"That's right." Melissa nodded toward him. "You might also remember that we had to let him go when the evidence went missing..."

He knew where this was going. And it wasn't going to be good.

Not for anyone.

"The suspect was told not to leave town but disappeared within an hour of having been released."

He remembered that, too, now that she mentioned it. And missing evidence was what was tying this meeting to Randall Bowe.

Clarke had known Bowe for years and was disliking him more and more. He'd always had a snooty attitude, but recently the man had been accusing the Coltons of nepotism.

Teeth clenched, he listened as his sister continued, "This morning I met with Randall Bowe's lab assistant, who'd been blamed for the missing evidence and subsequently fired. She swears that she processed the evidence with all protocols observed. She double-checked it herself before she left that night. But when she came to work the next morning, it was gone…

"This morning another man in his fifties was found in the park, shot point-blank in the chest and posed with his hands folded over his abdomen."

And there it was. Feeling sick and angry at the same time, Clarke tapped his pen against his pad. Not lightly. Until Melissa glanced pointedly at the table where his notebook lay, and he stopped. Gritting his teeth instead.

"DNA evidence left at the scene of the second murder is a match for the Gully killing, even if we only have reports of the Gully evidence and not the evidence itself," she said. "We now have solid, not-missing, irrefutable evidence against the suspect in the Gully case—Len Davison—and no idea where to find him. He's obviously still close by, though. And ballsy, committing the exact same crime a second time on a second Grave Gulch citizen, right under our noses."

Everyone in the room sat back, glancing at each other. The others looked as stunned and disgusted as he felt.

"Randall Bowe has unleashed a huge load of crap and misery on this town and has to pay," Bryce said.

"Davison has to be stopped," Clarke said. First and foremost. He wanted Bowe badly, but at least they'd already taken away that man's ability to hurt them. But Davison…

"We've both been looking for Bowe," Troy told Clarke, motioning toward Bryce. "But so far have no actionable leads…"

"I'll get a team together and take on the hunt for

Davison." Bryce spoke up, sitting forward as though ready to spring into action. "We know he was an accountant, was laid off from his job at a large company, was an average employee. He has a daughter, Tatiana. We talked to her when Davison was a suspect for the first murder. I'd heard she went to Paris, but I'll see if I can track her down. With this looking like a serial case, the FBI should be the lead..."

"Fine." Melissa looked at the agent and nodded. "You get some officers together and deepen your search for Bowe. All overtime will be approved." She looked down the table to Clarke. "You mind doing some digging into the two victims? See if they have anything else in common besides their ages and walking dogs in the park? You can do that from your place..."

He gave her an immediate thumbs-up. Stood as the others did, eager to get home, but paused long enough to let the others depart before him.

"How's Everleigh holding up?" Melissa asked him as he shrugged into his coat, pocketing his notepad. Though tall and clearly strong, wearing her title with confidence, she still looked like his little sister to him, even in the way she held her folder of papers up to her chest.

"Better than you'd expect," he said. "She takes everything on the chin...but I know it's getting to her inside. Her grandmother's situation appears to be bothering her most of all. Is there anything you can do there?"

Her blue eyes shadowed with concern, Melissa shook her head. "Other than what I've already done...seen to it that she's housed with minimum offenders, and that she has all the perks anyone can get in prison...no. It's with the DA now."

He'd known what her response was going to be. Wasn't sure why he'd even asked. Nodding, he turned to go.

"Clarke?"

The authoritative tone in her voice had him turning back to her. She wasn't his boss. He was his own. But she hired him on a regular basis, and... "Yeah?"

He was used to the way she studied him. Held up to the scrutiny just fine. Until she said, "What's with you and Everleigh?"

"Nothing. Why?" He held her gaze, but it was tough.

"Your voice just sounds...different...every time she's mentioned."

"It's been, what, twenty-four hours since I met her? I'd hardly think that would give you time to assess a damn thing."

Oh, but he knew differently. Knew that the anger in his tone gave him away, to himself as much as Melissa.

"I don't think I've ever seen you be so protective with a woman that wasn't a member of our family."

He couldn't speak to that. Didn't go around assessing his levels of protectiveness.

"I'm just doing my job, sis," he said, attempting to calm himself with that truth. "Maybe it's not me that's different, but her. Everleigh accepts inequities in her life as though they're meant to be there, and yet she doesn't get bitter. Or hard. She just keeps moving forward. Doing the best she can. She's smart, maybe too loyal, if there is such a thing, but no matter what gets thrown at her, most of it unfairly, she doesn't complain…" He kept picturing her calmly returning more tackle than any one man needed to various boxes, knew he was saying too much. Told himself to wrap it up. "She was done wrong by the city of Grave Gulch. We owe her. And that's what this is. Me being extra vigilant in an attempt to pay her back."

All true.

And yet, as he quickstepped it out to his vehicle, he knew that he hadn't fooled Melissa. Or himself.

Chapter 9

Everleigh spent much of Friday on the phone with lawyers, bankers and insurance brokers. She canceled Fritz's remaining policies, and let the bank know she would no longer be paying for Fritz's sports car.

He'd driven it to the house just before he'd been killed. As far as she was concerned, the bank could come repossess it.

No one seemed to know if he'd come to the house alone that day.

There'd been no break-in the day of the murder, implying his killer had had a key or Fritz had let them in. That had been part of the rationale for blaming her. And due to the murder weapon and the type of injuries, they'd labeled it a crime of passion.

Clarke's thinking that the killer could have been one

of Fritz's mistresses made good sense. She'd far rather think that an unknown woman, rather than someone she actually knew, was behind this.

Clarke had texted to let her know that he was home less than an hour after he'd left. His brother was already gone, and other than the brief introduction, she hadn't seen or spoken to him. At noon, she went down and put together a chef salad for lunch, using her own groceries, texting Clarke to let him know that his was in the refrigerator if he wanted it.

And just after one, a good four hours before they had to even think about leaving for her mother's, he texted to ask if she was up to a trip to the apartment Fritz had rented for himself. She'd been planning to visit the small place, to clean out his stuff, after grocery shopping the day before. The estate lawyer had told her that Fritz had paid six months' rent up front, so she had time, but…

The police have already been over it, sweeping for DNA, Clarke texted her, but I'd like to go back and see if you and I together can find anything that might tell us where to look for any of the women he'd been sleeping with.

He was working the case. And because that felt good and right to her, she sent back immediate agreement, hitting Send as she left the lovely room she'd been allotted.

Nervous about venturing out. About being in Fritz's space—somewhere she'd never been, but maybe his killer had. And most nervous of all about spending the afternoon, as well as the evening, with a man who sent way too many vibes for her to avoid.

* * *

Clarke was driving a loaner vehicle, a black town car with tinted windows that looked like something a mobster would drive, while the back passenger door of his SUV was being repaired. He'd paid extra for the rental car, having it delivered late that morning. After that shot had been fired at them, he couldn't contemplate driving Everleigh around in a car that left them both sitting ducks. He knew she wouldn't agree to be a total prisoner. He'd suggested as much the day before to no avail. She was going to visit her gram. And they needed to go to the party that night. She wanted her life back. And she was going to do whatever she had to do to make that happen…with him at her side.

So he took her to Fritz's apartment, and out they were, but at least anyone outside the car wouldn't be able to see her head through the window to properly take aim…

He had to assume that whoever was after her was everywhere she was. It was the only way to keep her safe.

And while he also knew that luring the person out was the quickest and best way to find the perp, using Everleigh as bait went against every single instinct in his body.

Everleigh had the key to the apartment on her ring, and as cold as it was, no one was outside in the quiet neighborhood when she let them inside. Looking around the place itself proved as uneventful as the trip over had been. Furnished with nondescript pieces, the three rooms looked more like a middle-line hotel suite than anything else. Other than clothes in the closet and a few of the drawers, a phone charger and toiletries, there was nothing else there.

"He came home every day I worked," Everleigh reminded him. While she watched silently, he turned the place over pretty thoroughly anyway.

Just because there was nothing of him there didn't mean a woman hadn't lost something along the way. Happened during affairs in hotel rooms all the time.

"An earring back, even, could be a clue," he said, pulling the sheets down off the bed. As though she'd only been waiting for direction, Everleigh started pulling out drawers, in the bedroom and the adjoining bath. Looking in the shower, on the floor by the toilet...anyplace anything small could have dropped.

And as much as Clarke wanted to be immune to Everleigh, the way she took all of this on—without what would have been perfectly understandable histrionics, or even the edge being in that place should have given her—had him admiring the hell out of her instead.

She wanted out. Of the apartment. Of the need for protection. Of any talk of murder. So Everleigh went to work. Trying not to think about the fact that Fritz had traded eighteen years of marriage to her for the boring little generic apartment and affairs with someone else.

So yeah, Clarke Colton might find her intriguing, but he'd known her only a day. She couldn't let herself make anything of it. Everleigh refused to risk ever being in a vulnerable position like the current one again. She'd get through the moments ahead, one at a time, and she was going to build a good life that depended only on herself and never look back. She'd seen enough of the past.

"I talked to Melissa about your grandmother," Clarke said as they went through kitchen drawers—him on one end of the little kitchen, her on the other.

She looked over at him, hands frozen. "And?"

A shake of his head had her going back to work. "It's like she told you—it's with the DA. There's nothing more she can do. You have to convince her to take a plea, Everleigh. It's the only way she's got a hope of getting out in a reasonable amount of time."

His words got her ire up. Didn't matter if they were accurate or not. Didn't even matter the guise in which they were offered. She didn't care if he was trying to be kind, to help. She was not going to just accept that her gram might die in prison.

And because of her…

"I'm holding out hope," she said, her strong tone driven by the tension inside her. She shut one drawer a little harder than necessary and moved on to silverware. "It worked for me. My case was a slam dunk. Everyone was certain I was guilty. And I got out. I've got faith that something will come up for Gram, too."

"There's a major difference here." He'd stopped at a utensil drawer, his head turned toward her. She saw him with peripheral vision but didn't face him.

"What's that?"

"Hannah's guilty, and she admitted it," he said. "You weren't and didn't."

She couldn't let him build doubt to the point of giving up. If Gram had given up on her when all seemed lost, Everleigh would be spending her life in prison.

"I know she's eighty years old," he said softly. "And I know she had good reason for what she did. Her cause was right. The police were wrong, and she had to prove that. All of those mitigating factors will help her, certainly, but she's still a kidnapper..."

"She wasn't stealing him. She was just getting your family's attention in the only way left to her. None of you would listen to her. You were all so certain that I was a murderer..."

Yeah, she was still a bit bothered by that. She understood that the evidence concocted by Bowe had looked bad, but once they'd seen what he'd presented, they'd stopped looking. In spite of the fact that a crime-scene investigator had relayed the evidence differently.

"She took him, Everleigh. With reason that was sound to her, with good intentions, maybe, but without permission."

"Why don't we just wait and see what happens?" she said, getting increasingly agitated and not wanting to make a fool of herself. Who did he think he was, sitting as judge and jury on her grandmother before there'd even been a trial?

Even if he was right in the end, she was right to hold on to hope. He could not to take that from her.

"She needs to take a plea," he said again. Not letting it go. "You're trying to justify vigilante justice and we can't live together in society with that kind of thinking," he said, almost as though lecturing a class, and she wondered if he was trying to piss her off on purpose.

Or maybe he'd had enough of her. It couldn't be easy for a guy like him to have a constant companion around his neck, invading his home, twenty-four hours a day.

She'd tried to stay out of his way…

"I'm not saying we can take matters in our own hands just because we don't like the way the system is working, or not working, in a particular instance," she said, trying not to grit her teeth. She bit back a string of words best left unsaid. "What I *am* saying—" pain made her voice a bit stronger than it should have been "—is that I'm hoping something neither one of us can see right now will present itself and the situation will be resolved. There are still protests going on downtown. You have to have seen them when you went to the station this morning…" She'd seen them on the news she'd watched on her tablet. Had cried a little at the sight of so much support for her gram.

"We can't rule by popular opinion, either," he said. "We've got laws for a reason. Without them we all live in chaos…"

He just wasn't able to get it. Didn't seem to comprehend what hope was all about. And she kind of understood. He was the oldest of his generation in a large successful family and hadn't had to grow up dreaming of a better life as she had. And the law-and-order part—she got that, too. But he might want to take note… The townspeople weren't real happy with the way the GGPD was being run as of late.

Still, she needed Clarke's help. And Gram had taught her a long time before not to bite the hand that fed her. She wanted to stand up for hope. To show him there was more than just thought and facts. But when she realized why, realized she was taking his attitude personally, she stopped. "I respect the law, Clarke," was all she said.

And set about searching cupboards for any sign of her deceased husband's lovers.

Or any other reason someone would want them both dead.

What in the hell was the matter with him, picking a fight with Everleigh just so she'd see reality and not get hurt again? His job was to protect her person, not her heart. If she wanted to believe that someone could wave a magic wand and set her grandmother free, then she had that right.

This lesson, that Everleigh's heart was not his to protect, had been a good one. Timely. Considering that in just a couple of hours they'd be on their way to her parents' house for a party that was bound to be emotionally stressful for Everleigh on so many levels.

And he didn't need to worry about how she felt, just keep her safe. He was there to investigate every single person who walked through the door. To make casual conversation all over the place. And see if he could figure out whom Fritz Emerson had been seeing. Either most recently or further back. Yeah, they were going to see her family, but she and Fritz had been married eighteen years; it stood to reason that Fritz would have developed relationships there. Maybe said too much during guys' poker night. And while Fritz and Everleigh had grown up in different neighborhoods, Grave Gulch wasn't all that large. And Fritz had supposedly chosen his women from the gym right there in town. Anyone could have seen him with any of those women. If his current mistress had been upset with Fritz for not filing divorce papers, that could be motive. And a jilted lover was always a prime suspect.

Feeling more like himself than he had since he'd run to the grocery store for a gallon of milk the morning before, Clarke was fine to ride in silence back to his place, where, he figured, Everleigh would return to her room, and he'd have another couple of hours to work. The lack of any apparent similarities between the cases Bowe had tampered with was bothering him. A lot. Why had the man manipulated evidence in only those instances?

Had the deed just been a compulsion that would come over him, like a sexual thrill? One he couldn't control?

The theory just didn't ring true with the scientist he'd known Bowe to be. He was meticulous about everything he did. Which meant he must have had specific reason for blowing those cases. For framing particular people. Or, conversely, as with Len Davison, the criminals he'd set free.

"Bowe didn't just get innocent people locked up," he said as they waited at a light several miles from his condo. Everleigh's silence had been starting to nag at him. He could tell she was upset, and he wanted to help. And Melissa had said, as she'd walked with him to the door of the station that morning, that he could tell Everleigh what he knew. As one of Bowe's victims, and a woman fighting for her life, she had the right to information.

"He didn't?" She'd turned to look at him, and with one brief glance, as their gazes connected there in that private front seat, his sense of balance flipped again.

There it was. That feeling that he could help her in more ways than one.

That she was calling out to him somehow.

That it was a call he needed to answer.

"He manipulated other cases where guilty people went free," he continued, steering himself with the course he'd chosen, trusting that the professional path was the best one. Working the case. Leaving the heart alone. Maybe when he was younger, women were more prone to just having fun, but hurting Aubrey as he had…not even knowing that she'd been starting to think they were going somewhere more than enjoying each other…she'd been devastated and he hadn't even seen it coming.

"There's one in particular…" He couldn't go into those details; they had nothing to do with her, and Melissa didn't want it to get out that there could be a serial killer in Grave Gulch. Not yet. She was hoping to catch the bastard before he had a chance to kill again. She didn't want to tip him off that they had him dead to rights.

"In fact, from what I've seen so far, they all had to do with murders…"

So, what was it that made Bowe lock up innocent people and let murderers go free?

"Do you know a guy named Len Davison?" he asked her. "Or Drew Orr? Maybe they were customers at Howlin' Eddie's?"

She shook her head. "I've never heard of either of them. Were they murdered, too? Or did Bowe meddle with their evidence?"

"I can't say, really. Orr is dead now, anyway—my

sister, Melissa, shot him in self-defense. Just wondered if you knew of either one of them."

"No. Could be they frequented the health spa," she offered. "Fritz used to keep a pretty good list of his clients—though, from what I've been told, recently they were mostly women. And not all just for his pleasure. He was particularly good with older women, patient, able to get them to stick to routines because he designed programs that were accessible, set achievable goals, and also because he made them feel good about themselves."

Again, there was no bitterness in her tone. Glancing her way as he finally got a green light and moved slowly forward in the traffic that had stacked up, Clarke wanted in. He wanted to know how she did it. How she stayed so…impartial. Seeming to see both sides to everything.

Except about her grandmother, of course.

"Do you mind if I have an officer swing by your house and pick up Fritz's computer so the GGPD tech guy, Ellie, can get a look at it?" he asked her.

"Of course not."

And while he was at it… "Will you also give me permission to search his phone records?"

"Yes."

Good. He'd have plenty of work to do to keep his mind busy—and off her—until party time.

The car's system was a little different from his own, and though he'd already paired his phone, he pushed the wrong button while trying to make a call and ended up missing his turn. Not a big deal, he could go around the block, just didn't like having Everleigh out any more than necessary. His course was firmly set as the shortest distance between two points.

He'd made the requests and hung up by the time he was able to right the error and make the correct turn. A red car, a newer-looking small SUV, turned when he did. Which was odd. It had been behind him, a few yards back, at the long light, too. During his time there, he'd taken an inventory of all the vehicles on all four corners. The odd thing was, he'd missed a turn. Was just doubling back. Why would someone else be mimicking his mistakes?

"Get down." The words were an unmistakable order.

Everleigh complied immediately, ducking first and then actually turning to her side and half lying on the console. Bringing her head close enough that he could feel a brush against his side. Resisting the urge to use his body to shield her, only because he needed both hands on the wheel, he quickly did an illegal U-turn and then turned again. He'd thought he'd lost the other car for a minute, when his continued rearview-mirror glances vetted nothing, but then it was there again. Several cars back. Too many for him to make out any kind of identifying markers. He knew it was the same vehicle, though, because the passenger sun visor was at an odd angle: halfway down. He couldn't make out a driver. Couldn't even see if the person was wearing a ski mask or not.

"We're being followed," he let Everleigh know. And put in a quick call to his sister, too. And then he just drove. Not to his place, or anywhere in particular. He stayed in traffic, in the downtown area, a part of the city with a lot of police presence, waiting for the car to be pulled over. But as soon as he'd passed the turn to his condo, the red SUV seemed to have disappeared. He'd lost it in traffic, behind a Chevy Suburban—a vehicle almost twice its size—and when his view was clear again, his pursuer was gone.

His concern was not.

Chapter 10

Everleigh's heart was still pounding as Clarke pulled into his condo garage. He'd had her stay down until they were safely inside, and she shot up as soon as he gave her the all clear, determining that she preferred to face what came head-on, not hide any more than she had to.

How could she hope to defend herself if she couldn't see what was coming at her?

She knew there were major fallacies in her argument—didn't want a bullet in the head, nor could she protect herself from one even if she saw it coming—but she'd just learned something about herself. She wasn't going to run away. She was going to stand and fight.

Even if that meant spending time in close quarters and a fake intimate relationship with a man who was wreaking havoc on everything she knew about herself. Or wanted for herself.

Clarke's phone rang before he'd even turned off the car. "Yeah," he said succinctly. "We're in, all good."

And then, as he was looking around them and unbuckling his seat belt, he added, "Good. Thanks. Let me get her inside and I'll call you back. We need to rethink her going to that party tonight."

Her. Her?

Like she wasn't a fully capable and functioning adult, in charge of her own life, sitting right there? Had he forgotten she'd hired *him*? Yeah, at his suggestion, coming from his sister, the chief of police. And, yeah, she needed his help. But…she had a say.

For the rest of her life, every breath she took, she would have a say.

And she was going to the party at her mother's that night.

Wise enough to understand that they needed their wits about them as they exited the car, and that the faster they got up to his place the better, she held her tongue until they were locked safely inside his condominium. And he did a quick sweep of the place.

Though, with the twenty-four-hour security of the building, she wasn't a bit surprised when he joined her at the base of the stairs to tell her that everything was fine.

She nodded, her hand on the banister, intending to head to her room to freshen up her makeup and fix her hair before heading out to her mother's.

"I have to call my sister back," he said as he stood

there, blocking her way. "And then we need to talk, so can you hang on a second?"

She could. But she wasn't going to. "No," she said. "And maybe you should think about talking to me before you call her back," she said, welcoming the anger that surged in place of fear. Anger felt…stronger. "You helping me might have been your idea, but I agreed to hire you. I'm paying you whether you want me to or not, and you can throw the money away if you wish…"

"We can talk about that later," he said, sounding a tad bit impatient. His tone didn't slow the rush of her anger a bit. Something else she noted as odd. Generally, the ire of others calmed her immediately. Like her job was to keep the peace.

She had something much more vital to focus on at the moment, though: her right to direct what happened in her own life.

"I'm not done," she told him. "I heard what you said in the car and I am going to the party tonight. Even if I have to fire you." Her gut lurched, knowing she meant the words. Knowing, too, the risk they put her in if he quit on her.

She just needed her own autonomy more.

"I don't want to fire you. I need your help. But you've said that you think Fritz's killer and whoever is after me could be there tonight. I need this to end. I need to get my life back and I need to be instrumental in doing that."

"What good is your life going to be to you if you're dead?"

"About the same as it is if I'm not in control of it."

His stare was not kind. Or gentle. It was pointed.

Searing. She didn't flinch. Or back away. In fact, her chin lifted a bit as she glared back at him.

"Are you telling me that you were wrong? That you don't think the killer will be there tonight?" she asked. "Or that you don't feel you have a good chance, the quickest chance, of finding out what's going on, if you're there?"

"No. But I might have misjudged the danger to you in going to the party," he said.

"And I might have misjudged the danger to you in hiring you," she shot back. "I'm like a time bomb and you're right beside me. If I explode, you could die, too. Or be badly hurt." It wasn't like he'd be any more capable of stopping a flying bullet aimed at them than she would.

His gaze softened, and as soon as she knew he relented, she deflated to the point of needing to sit down. She didn't, of course. She stood her ground as he said, "Fine, we'll go, but you follow my instructions the entire time or I'm out of there."

"That's fair." She *had* mentioned how his life was at stake, too, by association with her.

"I need to call my sister. We had a police escort into the garage, with them checking things out before we got here, and they'll want to arrange the same to and from the party tonight."

Everleigh secretly felt glad to know he wouldn't be on his own that night. It had just dawned on her, in the midst of this argument, that by helping her, Clarke really was putting his life in as much danger as hers was. She was also frightened all over again.

"All of this extra-man-hour pay just for me?" she

asked. The department owing her for a wrongful conviction was one thing, but two months out of a barmaid's life wouldn't amount to the kind of dollars the GGPD had seemed willing to spend on her behalf. People like her didn't rate attention like that. She wasn't even sure people like *him* rated that kind of spending. Grave Gulch was only so big, which meant that the police department had only so many resources. It wasn't like they were in some big fancy city that could produce extra personnel with just a phone call.

"Yes," he told her. "The department screwed up and they will make it right for you. It's bigger than that, too, and they want justice done, but the commitment to see you through to safety came before anyone knew that."

Bigger. He was referring to his meeting that morning. To the things he hadn't been able to tell her. But some he had…

"Because of Bowe."

"Yes. The FBI is involved now."

"And you're sure that doesn't have anything to do with why I'm in danger?"

His shrug might not have been much of an answer, but to Everleigh, the honesty in his reaction provided the reassurance she'd been seeking. "We can't be sure of anything until we have proof," he said. "But based on all evidence, there is nothing to point us in the direction of Bowe having targeted you for any particular reason. However, I am actively and diligently looking into any connections between you and others who were either hurt or helped by Randall Bowe."

She nodded. Satisfied.

And needed to get herself freshened up. It was going to be hard enough to walk into a room of traitors who claimed to love her—and who, she knew, did, but didn't trust her, people she loved but no longer trusted—without feeling like a used dishrag.

She wanted the filth of Fritz's bachelor pad off her skin. The scent out of her nose. If only she could wipe him out of the past eighteen years of her life as easily. Except that then she wouldn't be the woman she'd grown to be. Wouldn't be as strong. Wouldn't have spent her life helping to better and brighten the days of those who still lived in the neighborhood where she'd grown up.

In the past two months she'd gotten to know that woman better than she ever had before.

And wouldn't change who she'd become for anything.

Clarke did not have a good feeling about the evening ahead. He figured being there early would give him time to get a look at everyone in attendance—even those who didn't stay long.

In black jeans and a bulky off-white pullover sweater that would allow him to wear his gun without attracting attention to it, he'd put on the cologne he usually wore only when going out and his nicest ankle-high black leather boots, preparing for a tough night of work.

Starting the second he met up with Everleigh in the living room. She hadn't changed clothes but looked completely freshened up. The addition of big hoop earrings was a bit of a surprise. They gave her a louder, more adventurous look, but he liked it. Too much for the challenge he was facing.

He jumped right in. "We've got to make this…us together…believable," he told her, in a tone meant to brook no argument. Taking her to the party at all was costing him greatly, with his instincts hammering at him to lock her in the condo. Protective instincts he hadn't known he had were suddenly popping up faster than he could shoot them down. "If whoever is after you is there, they'll be more watchful than you'd expect. And we already know whoever it is is taking risks we wouldn't expect, not thinking rationally… There's no telling what they might do if provoked…"

He didn't like scaring her, but he liked it better than her being dead.

"Your husband's only been gone a couple of months. You've been in jail for pretty much all of that time. If we expect anyone to believe we're together, we have to get our story straight and then live it as though it's real."

She'd been married eighteen years. Hadn't kissed another man in all that time until the day before. The fact that she actually had kissed Clarke back worked in their favor. He needed her to convince others that being with him made her different…made her want to date again. Whatever had prompted her to move her mouth against his could go a long way in convincing her family that she really had feelings for Clarke.

And that kiss had complicated his plan to keep an emotional distance between them. He'd dreamed of her the night before. And had woken up hard.

Twice.

But the plan to get past that was not impossible. He hoped to God, anyway.

The fact that he'd been the first man she'd kissed in that amount of time, other than the slime who'd done her so wrong, brought out the he-man in him. The one who wanted to claim her and take her to bed and show her how good he could help her feel. And the fact also made him nervous as hell. Could a woman who'd been faithful for so long, even after her husband had moved out, pull off the fiction of a sudden love affair?

She hadn't said a word. Was watching him, though.

"What?" he asked. Trying to prepare for whatever argument she was working up was exhausting resources he needed to keep her alive.

"I'm just waiting for the story," she said, her tone soft. Almost gentle. "I told you that you call the shots, that I follow instructions. I'm going to the party as I need to do. The rest is yours."

His mouth fell open—mostly because he opened it to speak and nothing came out. Just when he thought he had her figured out, she threw him off balance again.

"It would be best if we come up with the backstory together," he explained. "That's what I was after. These people know you. You need to tell me how it is that you've come to be involved with me, describe us to me as you would see it. That's the only way we'll be able to get people who've known and loved you your whole life to believe us."

Her snort wasn't ladylike, but it was damn cute. The look in her eye wasn't as she said, "Are you kidding me? The GGPD say I'm a murderer and they were convinced just like that..."

He swallowed back the compassion that arose. And said, "This is different, Everleigh. You've been through a lot. They let you down. Those who truly care about you are going to be watching you closely, and being extra careful around you, wanting to help..."

She shrugged. Adjusted the skinny long strap of the small purse she had on her shoulder and reached for the coat she'd left on the freestanding rack at his front door.

"We met while I was in prison," she told him. "You didn't believe I committed the murder and came to see me. That's why, when the GGPD took another look at the case, they gave you access to Bowe's files, and since you'd already studied the evidence collected by CSI, you were able to help prove the discrepancy. We were already developing feelings for each other while I was in prison, and when I got out, things escalated quickly. You've made me feel more alive than I've ever felt in my life. And bring out emotions in me I didn't know I had."

His mouth dry, Clarke couldn't swallow, let alone reply. His entire body was on alert, his penis growing, his heart pounding.

"You asked what would convince them," she said, buttoning her coat over her purse. "If you don't like my fairy tale, make up one of your own, tell me what you want me to say, and I'll sell it to them. I really don't care about the story, Clarke. I just want to get there and get this over with."

Right. She'd been coming up with a story she

thought her family would believe. Not bringing his previous night's fantasy to life in stunning clarity.

What in the hell was the matter with him? He'd been asking himself that question way too often since she'd come into his life and he'd better find an answer quick. And then fix whatever the problem was.

"I think your story is good," he told her, covering his groin with his own coat. Grabbing his keys. "Whatever you'd say, that's what we need. Something that comes from you."

No way he could come up with anything else at the moment. And truth was, if he'd believed her there for a moment…actually thinking that she'd suddenly chosen that moment to confess what she'd been feeling since their kiss the day before, as though its memory had been haunting her life, too…when he knew it to be a lie…then chances were good her family and friends would believe her.

In the elevator, he stood right next to her, and when the car started downward, he put an arm around her shoulders, hugging her to him. She stiffened immediately.

And in spite of her reaction, so did his penis.

"Actions are much more believable than words," he told her. "No matter how good the story is, if we don't touch, or if you stiffen when we do, this whole thing is going to fail."

"Point taken," she said, sliding an arm around his waist, sending him into an immediate image of her pressing him up against the elevator wall and having her way with him.

It was then that he knew she wasn't the one he needed to worry about. Nor was her family.

He was the one who was failing in the acting department, failing to appear like he didn't have feelings for Everleigh. But he'd die before he failed to keep her safe.

Coming from Clarke's condo and knowing what she did about his family, Everleigh found herself embarrassed as they pulled up in front of her parents' clean, but clearly aged-and-not-in-a-good-way home in a neighborhood of older, not-updated homes with small yards filled with snow that covered the cracked sidewalks. Shivering, she didn't know what Clarke was seeing, but her gaze went straight to the broken shutter, top left. It had been that way her whole life. Used to be how she'd pick her house out from down the street of identical-looking skinny shotgun-style homes that lined the block.

The piece of black metal blurred as tears filled her eyes. This place looked like home, but it didn't feel that way to her. That porch…the outside lights that gleamed from both sides of the door to welcome guests… None of it glowed with love anymore.

They'd come early purposely, before the other guests arrived, so that she could get through the initial moments of seeing her parents for the first time since she was arrested without an audience. But when she saw the front door open, framing her mother and father—and also her aunt and a couple of other bodies she couldn't see well enough to identify—her heart sank.

"Do they know you're bringing a guest?" Clarke

asked from beside her. His calm tone, as though they were discussing how they wanted their burgers cooked, seemed to lighten the tension in her chest a small bit. Allowing a bit more freedom in her lungs.

"Yeah. I told Mom that we're seeing each other and asked if I could bring you along. That's the way it's done here," she added. "You ask…"

"What would you have done if she'd said no?"

She glanced at him, feeling the early evening's chill in the air as he turned off the car. "She'd never say no," she told him. "Any friend I ever wanted to bring home was welcome."

As an only child, she'd been well loved. Or so she'd thought.

But then, she'd thought she'd been loved and honored as a wife, too…

Given the onlookers' presence, he told her to wait for him to come around to get her. Giving him the appearance of being the perfect gentleman to his date. She figured he'd really issued the order more as a bodyguard than a lover. Either way, she was happy to comply.

She wanted him there. And wanted the evening over. They had to get on with it.

Everleigh knew why Clarke's arm was around her waist as they traipsed through the snow up the covered walkway and to the porch. But her body melting into him wasn't just because of the show they were putting on. For those few seconds, right or wrong, she leaned on his solid warmth.

She was potentially walking into the presence of someone who wanted her dead.

"Baby girl!" Amie McPherson came bursting out the door, medical boot and all, as soon as they reached the porch, pulling her close for one of her tightest hugs. Embraces that Everleigh used to soak up. That used to make her feel loved.

The effusiveness seemed over-the-top after her mother had sold her up the river to the police when they'd come calling, saying she must be a murderer. Maybe the hug was for the benefit of the audience standing behind them.

Everleigh pulled away quickly. "You don't have a coat on, Mom," she said, using the cold as an excuse as she reached for Clarke's hand and took a step toward the door and all of the people waiting there. She moved past them. Or rather, kept moving and they got out of the way. It was either that or have her bump into them. She wasn't going to break into tears in front of everyone, and that left her with no choice but to stand on her anger for the moment. Her aunt was just inside the door and stepped back as her parents did, forcing the other few people there—some close neighbors, explaining a lack of cars outside—to step back as well, and she pulled Clarke inside.

"This is Clarke Colton," she said. "And, yes, he's brother to the chief of police, but he's not a cop. He's here as my date and I would appreciate it if you'd treat him accordingly. He's not working, he doesn't answer for what his sister or the rest of the department does, and I want him to be able to get to know my family and friends the way I do."

There. She hadn't planned the speech. Or any greeting. She'd been dreading seeing her mother more than anything.

Her father stepped forward, his pants and plaid flannel shirt looking like his best, as he gave her a hug. "Good to have you home, Missy," Andrew McPherson said, using his nickname for her. Warming her heart for a brief second.

Until she remembered that he hadn't stood up for her, either. He hadn't blamed her. Had tried to come to her defense in terms of never having really liked Fritz or the way he'd treated her.

But...after being presented with DNA evidence, he'd believed her capable of taking a life.

She just couldn't wrap her mind around that. Yeah, it looked like the evidence proved her guilt, but faith was believing without, or in spite of, proof.

Neither of her parents had faith in her.

And someone still wanted her dead.

While she grappled with an overwhelming sense of grief, Clarke stepped forward, still holding her hand, but greeting the others, shaking their hands...starting with her dad first and then her mother.

The doorbell rang a minute or two later, and Amie herded everyone to the back through the entryway to the living room and then on to the kitchen. Guests could mingle in the two rooms, able to access the bathroom off the kitchen, for the remainder of the night. The bedrooms upstairs were off-limits.

It was the way things were done.

The way they'd always been done in the world in which she'd grown up.

It just didn't feel like her world anymore.

And she most definitely didn't feel safe there.

Chapter 11

Clarke didn't want to let go of Everleigh. He wanted to hold her. To keep a hand on her back.

He just plain wanted to touch her.

To protect her, but also because he liked the way contact with her made him feel. Too much.

For that last reason, he distanced himself from her as soon as they got into the living room. He stayed close—no one was going to get a chance to hurt her—but he was never going to be a clingy man. Not even if hell froze over and he fell in love and got married someday.

The likelihood of that had never even crossed his mind before. So why in the hell was it doing so standing in the McPhersons' somewhat dingy, but clean and uncluttered living room? Picturing a Christmas tree in front of the large window and a little girl in flannel pj's with sassy blond hair, eyes all aglow as she stared at the packages beneath the colorfully lit tree.

Shaking his head, he took inventory of the people at the party. They were pouring in by the threes and fours. All ages. Genders. All seeming to know each other well. Several pretty young women who could have attracted Fritz's attention.

"Everleigh tells me you're the one who got her out of prison." An older man in a flannel shirt and jeans held up by suspenders took a step closer to Clarke, beer in hand, as he spoke.

"I helped find the discrepancy in the evidence," he said. "But only because I'd already been talking to her and knew what to look for," he added, wishing he had a beer to sip as well to ease the tension. There was plenty to go around, stacked up on a portable bar in the corner, but he didn't drink on the job.

"Yeah, well, I'm glad she had you for a friend," the man continued. Never told Clarke his name, but this man was already acting as though they were best buds. "Our Everleigh, she's always been a sweetie, too quiet and kind for her own good around here, I used to think. Way too good a girl for that slick bub she married," the bald man continued. "Her folks, they went on and on about him and how he moved Everleigh uptown, but I knew he was no good."

"How'd you know that?" Clarke asked in his role of investigator. He hoped. Waiting for the answer with an interest that seemed to border on personal.

"I saw him over in Ann Arbor once, walking with a beauty ten years younger than him, even after he married Everleigh. But I knew for sure last year when my girl came home and told me he was screwin' around with the cousin of a friend of hers. The cousin was visiting, went to his health club, and the two of them hit it off. From what I heard, they were a thing for a while after the cousin left to go home to Grand Rapids. He used to travel up to see her."

"And you didn't think to let Everleigh know?" The indignant question came out when he should have been asking the woman's name.

"Wasn't my business," he said. "Besides, I didn't see it myself…and for all I know, she knew what he was up to. Some women turn a blind eye to a husband's philandering…"

Not happily. Not that Clarke had ever heard. "You got the girl's name?" he asked. "Just in case someone else mentions her to Everleigh…"

"Nah. Annabelle, I think. But… Wait. Yeah, it was Annabelle Belinski. I remember because I had a friend named Belinski years ago. Used to go up to the UP hunting together."

UP. The upper peninsula of Michigan. Rugged territory. And highly popular with outdoors people, too. Clarke immediately started talking about a snowmobile trip he and his brothers had taken in the northern country years ago, how they'd almost lost toes to frostbite, crashed into snowbanks and generally had the time of their lives.

Annabelle Belinski. The name would go in the notebook tucked into his coat pocket as soon as he had the ability to put it there without being seen.

* * *

"I swear to God, baby, I never thought you were a murderer. Never believed you could have killed anyone, let alone your own husband. But they were shoving scientific DNA proof under our noses, like I was supposed to explain how it could be there and you not be guilty, and I didn't know how." Amie's hazel eyes, so much like Everleigh's own, were moist as she held her daughter captive in a corner of the living room, her whispers filled with intensity. "Then that day they came to the house after the kidnapping that was supposed to free you… I said I didn't recognize your grandmother. I didn't want them to find that baby until they'd taken another look at your case. I didn't know how else I could help."

Everleigh didn't respond. Wanted to look away but just couldn't quite get there. Her mother was her mother. She'd birthed her. Raised her. Everleigh couldn't help what she believed, either, and at the moment, she didn't know if she believed her mother. It hadn't just been the words Amie had said back then about DNA evidence convincing her of her daughter's guilt—but in the actions. In the two months she'd been in jail, her mother hadn't visited. She'd been in the courtroom for her trial, but she hadn't been at the prison gate the day she'd been released.

Supposedly she'd been busy with a protest to have Gram, her mother-in-law, released from jail.

And Everleigh never should have lingered near the corner by the piano. She'd been watching people come in. Wondering as each face came through the door if that person could be the one who'd tried to kill her.

As though she'd get some vibe when she saw them face-to-face.

She'd gravitated toward the corner to cover her back. Ironically, she was finding a semblance of safety in the spot that had been designated for her time-outs when she got in trouble as a little kid.

"I didn't stand up for you the day Gram took the baby because they'd been looking at me for kidnapping." Amie leaned in closer, her whispers grew more strident, and all Everleigh wanted to do was scoot between her mother and the old piano she'd taken lessons on so many years ago and break free into the room where thirty or more people were lingering.

"The only motive was forcing them to take another look at the case, and if I believed you did it, why would I steal a child to get them to look again?" She was talking now, as opposed to sounding rasping in a raised whisper, as the noise in the room increased with more people arriving. Everleigh hadn't made it out to the kitchen yet. Hadn't had dinner.

Didn't really want any. The imploring look in Amie's gaze grabbed at her. Like a suffocating claw. And in grief, too.

Her mother was trying to comfort her, to show her love, but all Everleigh could see was that her mother had been reluctant to believe the DNA evidence could be wrong.

Where had Amie been during the two months Everleigh had been sitting in jail? Maybe not totally believing her daughter was a murderer, but she hadn't stood up for her, either. Hadn't supported her as Gram had.

She knew where her dad had been. Futzing around

the house now that he was retired from the factory, and on his regular stool at the pub on the corner. Drinking his beer.

"I love you, Everleigh. You're my life..."

She nodded, needing to get away so bad she was ready to push her mother aside but for the chance that the woman would draw her into another hug.

And for the fact that she didn't want to hurt her mom. She still loved her. And knew her mother loved her, too. It had never been about the love.

Glancing up, she saw Clarke just off to her mother's left. Clara, the lady who lived across the street, was talking to him, but one glance from Everleigh and he was close enough to Amie to reach beyond her for Everleigh's hand, pulling her out slowly, causing Amie to naturally step aside.

"Clara tells me you used to take ballet lessons at the local family center," he said, and then included Amie in his glance. "Is that true?"

As Amie smiled at the two of them, regaling Clarke with the story about Everleigh being the only one in her four-year-old class who'd remembered the whole dance routine during her first recital, he leaned in and kissed Everleigh on the cheek.

It meant nothing, she knew.

But standing there, clutching his hand like the lifeline he'd just offered her, availing herself of the breather from the emotional distress her parents' defection had caused, she could have sworn his affection was real. That he'd saved her because he cared for her, not because he was working.

Which scared the crap out of her.

She couldn't even tell when someone was being honest anymore.

Had she ever been able to do so?

How was she ever going to trust herself to know?

Clarke didn't provide any answers. How could he? But when he slid his arm around her and walked her over to say hello to Clara, she allowed herself the distraction being close to him offered.

Even if it was the wrong thing to do.

He could feel her fear. Clarke might not have known Everleigh for long, but after spending two full days in her company, in very trying circumstances, he'd learned enough to know that she was struggling.

She smiled as she introduced him. Was great at parrying congratulations on her release and bringing the conversation away from herself and to her grandmother's plight, wanting everyone to continue to support her gram in any way they could. To write letters to the GGPD. He could have told her that wouldn't do any good but didn't.

She asked after ongoing situations in neighbors' lives, chatted with her aunt, talked to her dad about having visited his mother the day before, urging him to go himself.

And a good bit of the while, she was clutching Clarke's hand, as though she'd fall down if she let go.

While her gaze darted around the room.

She'd even jerked against him a time or two when the front door opened, signaling another new arrival.

When they made it to the kitchen and she moved around the spread of food there, she seemed to relax some. He stood by her as she put veggies on a plate, and then he leaned in, nuzzling her neck, to whisper, "You're doing great."

He knew he'd never forget her grateful smile. He just knew it.

And as they found a hallway wall to lean against while they ate, he was able to ask, "Have you noticed anything about anyone? Got any sense that anyone is treating you differently?"

She shook her head. "I'm getting obsessed, wondering if that person is here," she said. "Maybe this wasn't the right answer. Maybe whoever is after me isn't even here. Isn't someone close to me after all."

Thinking of Annabelle Belinski, he shrugged. "That's certainly possible," he agreed. "I need to move around a bit more. Talk to some people without you right next to me so I can casually start a conversation about Fritz and maybe find out who he'd been seeing. People would figure me for being curious, wouldn't find it odd, me asking about your ex, but with you standing right there..."

She nodded. Threw the paper plate into the trash with the rest of her dinner. And walked off without another word.

He watched her going, feeling a bit too much like the lovesick pup he was pretending to be.

Had she piled it on too thick? Or somehow given him some vibe that she was leaning on him more than she should have been? Reddening at the idea that Clarke Colton had had to tell her to give him some space, Everleigh entered the living room with trepidation, determination and a strong desire to get out of her parents' home, their neighborhood, and just keep going.

To build a completely new life.

She no longer fit the old one.

Feeling completely alone, more than she'd have ever thought possible, she pasted a smile on her face and made her way slowly through the throng of people in the living room, stopping to talk on Gram's behalf several times, encouraging people to write to her, to help keep her spirits up. Having just come from two months behind bars, she knew how important it was to have contact with loved ones. To feel like there was still a life for you on the outside.

Clarke kept her in his sights. She looked up a few times to see him just feet away, in conversation, but watching her, too. And warmed up a tad. They weren't a couple. The relationship they were presenting at the party was fake. But he was real. And in her life at the moment.

The bridge to get her from who she was into a safe place to become the woman whose skin she was growing into.

"Everleigh!" Turning, she saw a bright spot in the room, opening her arms for Larissa and returning the tight hug. The blonde, a little taller than Everleigh with blue eyes and perfect skin, had been out of town taking care of her sick mother since Everleigh's release.

"God, girl, it's so good to see you," Larissa said, giving her another quick hug before looking her over from head to toe. "I told you those boots would do it."

Smiling, Everleigh nodded. "How's your mom?" Larissa's mother refused to leave the house in Grand

Rapids where her daughter had grown up. And so Larissa made regular treks back now that her mother was widowed.

"Good. Better. Turned out it was just a bladder infection. I told you I'd make it back in time for the party."

Yeah, well, she'd been told a lot of things, and found herself not counting on any of them until they happened.

Finding a somewhat quiet space along the wall by the television, she pulled Larissa with her and caught up on everything that had been going on at Howlin' Eddie's in the past two months. And heard about Larissa's married younger sister and her seemingly perfect husband, too. The pair, who both had high-powered jobs in DC, were expecting their first child. Larissa couldn't wait to be an aunt.

And Everleigh knew that being the older sister working in a bar, not married and without children hurt Larissa, too. Like Everleigh, Larissa had married the wrong man. But unlike her, Larissa had divorced him years ago.

"So tell me about your hunky boyfriend," Larissa said, grinning as she glanced at Clarke and poked Everleigh in the shoulder. "You've been holding out on me!"

Everleigh shook her head. Was not going to give any misconceptions that could lead people to think that she really had been cheating on Fritz. Fixing the damage he'd done to her reputation was on her…even as she had to pretend that she and Clarke were together.

"I just met him while I was in prison," she said,

managing to look her friend in the eye while she lied. Hating that she managed to pull it off. She wasn't a liar.

Or a cheater, either. Looking at Clarke, she found a resurgence of strength, a reminder of why she was there, doing what she was doing. There was a murderer on the loose—and she was helping to catch them.

She had to stick to her story. To keep Clarke safe, as well as herself.

"He's like no man I've ever known," she said, the words pouring out of her because they had to. "He touches me and it's like you read in books… I physically melt. I never knew such a thing was possible…"

She was telling a story to save her life. And his.

She needed people to believe her.

And to remind herself that no matter what truth might seep through, no matter how relieved she suddenly felt saying something out loud that she'd been avoiding admitting, there was no truth in her being Clarke Colton's girlfriend. Or in him being her man.

"I heard about the break-in at your house, the ransacking," Larissa said, her voice lowered, as though she also thought someone in the room could be the perpetrator of the crime. "Does he have anything to do with finding out who did it?"

Everleigh shook her head. It wasn't the first time that night she'd heard the question. Apparently, everyone knew about the break-in.

But no one had mentioned the near murder in the grocery-store parking lot.

"He's a private investigator, not a cop," she told Larissa. That part was just fact. And easy. "He'd been helping me with my case even before Gram's kidnapping. Which was why he was able to help find the discrepancy in evidence so quickly when the police asked him to look into my stuff." The lie rolled off her tongue. For him. He was risking his life for *her*.

Yeah, it was his job. Yeah, if he wasn't working on her case, he could be on another that put his life at risk, but she'd given him her word. And he was trusting his life to her keeping her word.

"So, what's he think about the break-in?"

Larissa's concern was so sweet. Real. Which made lying to her so hard. She shook her head. "The police are working the case still," she said. "From what I've been told, they have no idea who's behind it." There. She'd found a way to be truthful. And felt better.

"Have you been back in the house?" Larissa asked.

She nodded. "As soon as the police were done with it. I couldn't leave it a mess," she said and grinned. "You know me. I need my space orderly." They'd joked about the fact that Everleigh was one barmaid who'd always kept their shared station clean and tidy.

"Aren't you nervous about staying there?"

She shrugged. Didn't look at Clarke that time. She'd failed to factor in how difficult it would be to lie to a real friend when she'd walked into the plan with Clarke that evening. And didn't know how much about her current living situation she could divulge.

"So, come stay with me," Larissa said, giving her hand a squeeze. "Seriously, I'd love having you. I've got the spare room just sitting there empty...

"You can bring Forester," her friend added.

For a second there, a long second, Everleigh was tempted. Most particularly because she was still stinging from Clarke's need to tell her to give him space. Whether she'd been coming on too strong or not, his words had been a reminder to her. Because while she'd been hanging on him, she knew she hadn't just been acting.

The realization scared her in a way far different from someone making attempts on her life. Her attraction to Clarke could carry a much longer-lasting danger.

And yet the immediate peril…it was also real. And deadly serious. She couldn't expose Larissa to that.

"I'm fine where I am," she said. "But you have no idea how much it means that you offered." She looked her friend in the eye, appreciating Larissa's support. "But I have to take back my life, one way or the other…"

Larissa nodded, seemed a bit teary-eyed as she leaned forward and brushed a light kiss against Everleigh's cheek. "You know I'm always here for you," she said softly before she pulled back.

Everleigh did know. Larissa had had her back since the first day Everleigh had walked into Howlin' Eddie's dressed in her skimpy barmaid's outfit.

And she was grateful.

Chapter 12

Clarke had underestimated how many people would be at Everleigh's party. And how eager they'd be to talk to him—her new boyfriend—about her deceased husband. Seemed, now that the man was gone, they all had things to say about him. Many of them hadn't liked how he'd treated Everleigh, and he couldn't help but wonder if any of them had really stepped forward at any point during the past eighteen years to see if she needed help.

He admired Everleigh while she worked the room as though she owned it. She'd moved on past her friend from the bar almost two hours before, and even though many people had left and the party was dying down, she was still calling up enough smiles to make her seem at ease and happy enough to be there. She might be quiet. Gentle. But she had an iron rod for a backbone and took everything that came at her standing up. And with grace.

He'd heard too many people tell him about Fritz being seen with other women. Had just received a third name to check out when he saw Everleigh pull her phone out of the back pocket of her jeans and answer it.

Who'd be calling her at that hour? Most particularly, who'd be calling her at that hour if just about everyone she knew was in the house then?

Since he was there at the behest of the police department, any official calls could go through him…

When her brow tightened and her lips thinned, he went for their coats. Already had hers in hand, holding it out to her when she came toward him—and saw Amie and Andrew coming at them, too.

"That was my neighbor," Everleigh said before her parents reached them, taking her jacket from him. He'd moved quietly enough that most people in the room remained engaged in their conversations, seemingly unaware of what was going on around them. He wanted them to stay that way. "The one who has Forester. She saw someone snooping around the back windows of my house."

Her parents came up just as she said that last part, and Clarke, who already had on his coat, pulled out his phone. "I've got the police on speed dial," he told them. "And I'll keep her safe."

He didn't let them know he had a gun under his sweater.

With a hurried and obviously concerned request from the McPhersons to keep them posted of any possible developments, Clarke hurried Everleigh out to the car. He already had his sister on the line before he'd pulled away.

He stayed on the phone with Melissa until they were turning onto Everleigh's street.

Three police cars were already at the house by the time they pulled up. Though Clarke was itching to run, not walk, to the house to get inside, he parked between two patrol cars and stayed put. His job was to protect Everleigh first. To figure out who was out to get her, second.

"I guess this means it wasn't someone I know well," she said, her gaze never leaving her house as lights could be seen going on and off and officers searched every room.

"Unless it is. They could have an accomplice," he told her. She wouldn't want to hear what he was thinking, but he knew she'd want the truth. "Over half the people who were there had already left by the time you got the call. And they all knew you were going to be occupied for the rest of the night."

"I didn't get any vibes from anyone that they were after me. Or even resenting me."

He hadn't, either, to be honest.

He could tell her about what he *had* discovered, but held his tongue for the moment. Evidence of Fritz's philandering might prove crucial information, but at the moment, they needed to deal with what was going on at her house.

It wasn't long before Grace Colton, his rookie cop cousin, was tapping on his car window. With her blond hair pulled back in a ponytail and in her dress blues, he could almost begin to believe the twenty-five-year-old wasn't a kid anymore.

"It's all clear," Grace said, after a brief serious glance at him—almost as though daring him to smile at her. "Chief says you're free to go in, but asks that you don't touch anything until CSI can get here in the morning. Perp entered through the back door. There's some disarray, but we've searched the place, under beds, in closets… No one is there. The guess is that your neighbor saw the person leaving, not arriving."

He nodded. Thanked her. And absolutely did not crack a smile. He might remember when Grace had been in diapers, might even have changed her a time or two, but she'd earned her stripes since and deserved his respect.

Turning to Everleigh, he wanted to suggest that they head to his home—save whatever faced her at her house for the morning—but asked instead, "What do you want to do?"

Whoever was after her wasn't going away. And wasn't backing off.

He wanted her safely up in his condo, not out on a dark street, or in a home that had just been broken into.

"I want to go in."

"It might be easier in the light of day."

"I want to go in now."

Of course she did. She'd take it on and deal with it. Didn't matter if it was scary. Or dangerous. "You're sure?"

Her nod didn't surprise him.

The depth of his fear for her did.

* * *

She didn't plan to stay long. Had no desire to hang out at a house she was beginning to think she was going to sell rather than ever live in again for any length of time. But she had to see the damage for herself, assess what had happened so that she could factor it in with everything else as she tried to assimilate and figure out her new world. She had to step inside the space to reclaim her home from whoever had vandalized it.

Clarke was there to protect her as she did so, she knew.

She didn't kid herself about that one.

She'd still have gone inside, even if he wasn't. But without him, she'd have waited until it was light outside, and everything seemed less creepy.

As it was, Clarke seemed more inclined to linger than she was. A quick check through every room was all she'd wanted. He was checking out Fritz's den as though he was cataloging everything in sight.

"This room got most of the attention this time," he said, studying the place intently.

She'd noticed the same. The kitchen hadn't been touched at all, it seemed. Nor had most of the other rooms. Her bedroom drawers had taken another tumble. The mattress was pushed off the bed.

All was fixable in less than an hour.

There was no reason for tears to be pushing for release. Things had been much, much worse the day before.

"We have to figure out what his killer would be after. What got Fritz murdered." He shook his head.

"He owned a failing small health club and personal-training business. He had no partners and no enemies that I know of. We've been over this already," she told him, wanting the answers as badly as he did. Worse.

"I heard basically that same information echoed several times tonight." He was frowning, looking around, his gaze landing on the cabinet where she'd replaced the fishing tackle boxes.

And she was mentally swept back to the day before. On the floor. Moving her lips against his. Needing him. Wanting so much more. Wanting the touch of his hands.

Wanting to know where the kiss would lead, if culmination would be even half as good as that kiss had felt…

Shaking her head against the assault, she forced her focus back to his last words. He'd heard "basically" the same information.

Which implied that some information had been a little different.

"What else did you hear?" she asked him.

"Enough to know that my instincts are probably right on this one. My gut has been telling me all along that this is mistress related."

"So why kill him? Why does she want me dead? And what would she want here?"

His glance was direct. Personal. "Once I have those answers, this will be over."

She didn't want this over.

The thought ran contrary to everything she knew. Of course, she wanted it over. She wanted to be free.

To live without constant fear. To have her life back. To start her new future.

She just wasn't ready for her time with Clarke to end.

He'd lit a spark within her that she hadn't known was there. Made her feel things she truly hadn't thought possible. She'd been telling the complete truth when she'd described her feelings to Larissa earlier.

She had to know more about how Clarke's kiss had made her feel.

Didn't want to go forward until she knew where it led. Physically. Because other than that, she already knew it led nowhere. And had no intention of heading back into nowhere ever again.

Besides, if she couldn't trust herself to know whom she could put her faith in, any kind of a relationship beyond the physical was pretty much moot.

Didn't really matter, in any case. It wasn't like she'd go have sex just to see if it was as great as she'd thought it might be. To find out if she'd been missing out. If her lack of fire with Fritz hadn't been because of that floundering relationship.

Some women liked having flings. She wasn't one of them. Not even with a man like Clarke Colton, who seemed only too willing to just have fun with a woman.

Everleigh went upstairs the second they got home, not even stopping to hang her coat on the rack by the front door.

Figuring her choice to distance herself was for the best, considering that he'd spent the majority of the past several hours pretending to be in serious like with her, he dropped his coat on its normal hook, grabbed his little notebook out of the pocket and went straight to his office.

He'd never gotten around to making notes for himself that evening, but the night wasn't done, and neither was he.

At his desk, the first thing he did was write down the three names he'd been given that evening—all women that were known to have had sexual relationships with Everleigh's husband. It wasn't the first infidelity case he'd ever worked. Not by a long shot. As a PI, those jobs were about as common as butter on bread, but this one… It was kicking his gut.

That someone as kind and loyal as Everleigh had been treated so badly, so disrespectfully…

Watching her that night, he'd gained a whole new level of respect for her. He knew she was hurting still, and yet…there she'd been, for hours, smiling, being gracious, accepting congratulations without bitterness…all to fight for her grandmother's cause. Asking others to write to Hannah McPherson, to keep her spirits up, to visit her, he understood. But writing to the GGPD… All it was going to do was cause a mail-room clerk to process useless paperwork. Even if they wrote to the DA, the law was the law. People couldn't just let someone go because she was sweet and old and had committed a crime for a good cause. Law enforcement couldn't let someone off the hook because they were well liked.

Taking a chance that Ellie would be at her computer, even after ten on a Friday night, he texted the GGPD tech guru and wasn't surprised to get a response within seconds. Ellie worked more overtime than Clarke did, rarely seeing her boyfriend. It worked for the couple, though, since Mick Hanes worked ungodly hours, as well.

Clarke sent Ellie the three names he'd collected that evening, asking Ellie to work her magic and vet all three women, getting back to him as quickly as she could. Within half an hour she'd responded. Two of the women, including Annabelle Belinski, didn't show up anywhere but normal information databases.

The third—Brenda Nolton, a local woman—had a record for fraud.

Finally, he had something to go on, something that made sense—someone with a criminal record. A woman wanted for fraud could have easily been involved with a cheating, in-love-with-himself, thirty-something fitness guru, and it would make sense that she'd involved him in some scheme or vice versa. The venture might have gone wrong and she could have come after him. When he'd refused to make things right, what if she'd killed him? In rage or to get rid of him—either way, it made sense. And now maybe Brenda was after whatever she needed to get herself right with the venture gone wrong.

It was a solid theory. Something he could hang his hat on. Clarke took the stairs two at a time, slowing at the top only long enough to see that Everleigh's light was still on.

With his hand down low on the door, he rapped with the knuckles. He didn't want to startle her. Or command entrance, either.

"Yeah?" she called.

"You decent? I just got some information you might want to hear..." He had hope to offer her and knew how badly she needed some.

The lock on her door sounded—surprising him. She'd felt a need to enforce her privacy?

He took a step back.

The door opened.

And there she stood, looking like a dream he'd always wanted to have, blond hair tousled, ample breasts unfettered, and the rest of her pretty much a long, lean straight line, curves hidden within a pair of flannel pajamas.

Mouth open, he'd forgotten what he'd come to tell her.

She'd opened her door with one thought in mind... finding out what he knew. And in doing so opened a window to a whole new world. One where she was a free woman, not in prison, certainly, but not tied to anyone for anything.

And he was...just the most gorgeous man she'd ever seen up close.

A world where she was in her pajamas, bra off, getting ready for bed, and they were alone together in his home for the night.

Her boyfriend, as far as all of her friends and family thought. Already approved and accepted.

She could see in the window. Could feel herself in there.

Could feel a bubble encompassing them.

Wanted to just let it happen.

And said, "What did you find out?"

Her body parts were aching for him, though. And

a quick glance down—she'd been a married woman for a lot of years—showed her that at least one of his body parts was reactive, as well.

"Fritz was involved with a woman named Brenda Nolton. You know her?"

She shook her head. You'd think hearing about her husband screwing around on her, having a name put to a phantom person she'd known about, but he'd never admit to her face, would be like a cold shower in her bubble moment.

To the contrary. Her composure only made her want to get hot and bothered even more.

"She's from Grave Gulch," he said, as though knowing where the woman lived would somehow make Everleigh remember her. His gaze had locked onto hers and she couldn't make herself look away.

"I've never heard of her." Didn't want to know how Fritz had met her. When he'd seen her. How often. She just didn't care anymore. That life was gone. She just wanted to find out if Brenda was the one after her. She'd moved so far beyond Fritz Emerson that she was beginning to wonder how she'd stayed married to him for so long.

And to wonder if Clarke would kiss her again.

Would she kiss him back if he did?

And that was it? He'd come to tell her the name of… Wait…

"Is she the one who's after me?" she asked. "You think she broke into my house?"

He didn't so much shake his head as just duck it to the side a little. He didn't look away from her, either. If eyes could draw a soul out of a person, his might be doing it to her. She wasn't letting it go. But she wasn't stopping him from trying, either…

And then he blinked. And said, "I don't know yet, but she's at the top of my list. She's got a record for fraud," he said, going on to share his speculation about Brenda and Fritz. It made sense. Good sense.

Relief was heady, mixing in with the desire coursing through her. "Could this really be it?" she asked. Could they have found the culprit?

"It's a solid lead."

That was so Clarke. He wouldn't lie to her. Wouldn't get her hopes up too high, either, without the proof right in front of him.

And then she had another thought and came back to earth a tad. "If all that's true, where do I fit in? Why would she want me dead?"

"If he'd told her he was divorced, that he was going to marry her, or even getting divorced, and still hadn't filed the papers…that could be how he double-crossed her. This is a woman who served time in prison. She might be hardened. Got pissed. Lunged at him. And now the thought of you being free, the woman who came between her and her future…or, more likely, fearing that you'll find whatever it is that she's looking for in Fritz's office…"

"Unless she found it tonight. Maybe it's already over…"

Could it be that simple? Could she really be free?

Clarke took a step forward, his gaze suddenly changing from dark and intense to concerned. "Don't get too far ahead of yourself," he said. "She's still on the loose. And she has it in for you. If it's even her. It's not over yet." The warning in his tone was very clear. "I just wanted you to know that we've finally got something we can take a look at. I wanted you to know there's hope..."

His words almost made her cry. And she would have, if not for the heat she could feel emanating from him, engaging emotions that were far from sad. But his knowing she was hanging on to hope, rushing up to give her a shot of it... In nearly twenty years, Fritz had never done anything so kind for her.

He reached out a hand, brushed at the hair at her temple, just off her left eye. "Get some rest," he said, half turning toward the direction of his room.

If his hand hadn't been holding her head, she'd have nodded. Turned away. But he *was* cupping her head. His thumb lightly rubbing her temple.

Her lips were too dry. She had to run her tongue across them. He leaned in, glancing down at the movement, and she leaned, too. Just a little bit. He leaned a little more. She reached her mouth out, and he captured it. Touching gently for the first second.

And in the next, he was devouring her. Kissing hungrily. Wetly. Using his tongue in ways that sent spirals of tension to her nipples, her groin. And he wasn't the only one being aggressive. Her lips seemed to be moving in ways she'd never moved them before. Sucking at his lips. Pressing against him. Showing him what she needed.

He groaned, took a step closer...and she backed up. Just as he dropped his hand away from her.

What in the hell were they doing?

Mouth still open, her emotions raw, she looked up

at him. His eyes as intent as ever, he stared down into hers. “I have no explanation for that.” His tone was deeper, his breathing slightly ragged.

“None needed,” she told him, backing into her room and fumbling against the handle, closing the door between them.

And for the rest of the night, every time she woke up, all she could see was the unnerved look in his eyes as he'd stood there, completely still, while she'd shut him out.

Chapter 13

Clarke slept, but not as much as he had the night before. And only after a very long cold shower. After the third time waking up with a hard-on, he got up, made himself some coffee and got to work. He couldn't very well have someone go calling on Brenda Nolton at four in the morning, not without some evidence. He'd already sent an email to a colleague and fellow PI, a distant family member in Grand Rapids. Because all of the GGPD were so involved with everything going on locally, hunting a serial killer and a rogue CSI tech, he asked his relative to find out whatever he could on Annabelle Belinski, the only nonlocal woman on his list. First and foremost, if she'd been home over the past two days. Finding out if she had an alibi. Ellie was already checking on a warrant for Brenda Nolton's cell phone and credit-card records. And he sent a message to Melissa, too, keeping her apprised of what he'd done and asking for someone to just check out the alibi of the third woman on the list he'd sent to Ellie.

And then he dived into the other aspect of the case that was bothering him—why Randall Bowe had singled out Everleigh. What did she have in common, if anything, with the other cases they knew for certain the forensic scientist had manipulated?

He didn't think the current threat against Everleigh's life had anything to do with Bowe's interest in her case, but until he knew for sure, he wasn't going to rest easy, either.

He had access to all of Bowe's files and spent the next couple of hours poring over them—looking not at the evidence this time, but at the people wrongly convicted and now on trial. His first times through, he'd paid attention only to the evidence. To the proof that had been manipulated. Looking for some connection there. This time, he put all of that aside and just studied the people. Did a little techie work himself and looked up everything he could find on Drew Orr. Orr had been a former business associate of Melissa's new fiancé, hotelier Antonio Ruiz, before Orr had confessed to murdering his cheating girlfriend. But somehow the GGPD hadn't found enough evidence to convict Orr. Bowe had apparently made sure the evidence against him disappeared. That was before Orr came after Melissa, who'd had to shoot him to save her own life.

Then there was their new suspect, Len Davison. That man's file noted that, according to friends, neighbors and his daughter, he'd been a loving husband of almost thirty years, bringing his wife flowers every single Friday night after work. And he'd seen his wife through her terminal illness from cancer the previous year. He'd seemed the epitome of a loyal, faithful man. But the evidence had been irrefutable, hairs found at the scene giving them DNA evidence that had proved the killer to be Davison. In spite of that, Tatiana Davison, the man's daughter, had claimed Len was a loving spouse. A doting dad. And when the forensic evidence against him disappeared, he had to be set free.

Clarke looked at the victims of Bowe's crimes, too. The first, a cheating girlfriend. The perp went free. The second, a man walking his dog. No known motive for the killing. But the perp, a loyal husband and father, went free. The third—Everleigh's case. A cheating husband had claimed his wife had been the one stepping out on him, and evidence was fabricated to make the supposed cheating wife look guilty for a crime she didn't commit. She'd been charged and had gone to prison to await a trial that would have been a slam dunk if not for a courageous grandmother who'd given up her own future to have her granddaughter's innocence proved—something Bowe couldn't possibly have foreseen.

So, was Bowe behind the attack on Everleigh? Was he furious that his work had been undone and she was free?

But why ransack her house?

Why risk getting caught, now that he knew he'd been found out, by coming back to town?

It didn't make sense.

And didn't answer who'd really killed Fritz Emerson. It was much more likely that person knew that something was in Fritz's home, or suspected strongly that it was, and that Everleigh being free was putting her in the way of the perp getting it.

Besides, the forensic scientist wasn't a killer. He was an avenger of some sort…

But what did he have to avenge?

Clarke knew Bowe…couldn't think of anything that stood out in the man's personal life. He was married. Had been for a long time…

Longtime marriages. Cheating spouses. It wasn't about the crimes, for Bowe; it was about the people on trial. Could it be that infidelity was what drove the scientist?

Whether Clarke knew the motive or not, Bowe was already proved to have been the one to manipulate evidence in at least three cases.

He glanced at his watch. Six in the morning. With a softly muttered "to hell with it," he picked up his phone and dialed his sister.

And after a few words with her, he waited while she dialed in Troy.

"We've got the motive," Melissa said when Clarke had finished telling them what he'd figured out. That Randall Bowe fixed cases to make certain that allegedly cheating spouses paid. And those who'd been cheated on went free. Except he'd gotten it wrong with Everleigh—she'd been the victim, not Fritz.

He was defending marital fidelity and making those guilty of infidelity pay.

Bowe had set himself up not only as jury and judge,

but as God. Clarke wanted to kick the man into the next country and beyond.

"We've had officers canvassing various areas for Davison's daughter, Tatiana, in case she's come back from Paris," Troy offered.

Davison was gone. His daughter was gone. And Bowe was responsible for another killer being free.

"Get Stanton back over here and I'll go see Bowe's wife," Clarke said. "I'll see if she knows anything that could have triggered his obsession. And maybe get her to tell me something she won't tell detectives." It had worked for them in the past. And they needed Troy to stay on finding Bowe. And other GGPD manpower hunting for Len Davison. Those left were for him to put to use on the street for tracking down leads on Everleigh's attacker.

"You can call Stanton," Melissa told him.

"He'll listen better to you." He didn't have time to argue with her and hung up as soon as he'd said the words.

He'd heard movement upstairs.

Everleigh was awake.

In black jeans, a purple sweater, her boots and purple drop earrings, Everleigh barreled down the stairs. As soon as she'd hung up the phone from her daily morning check on her grandmother, she'd showered in record time and was heading out. Gram wasn't feeling well.

Clarke was up already—good. She hadn't known. "I have to get to the prison," she said. "To see Gram."

"Visiting hours don't start for another three hours."

"Yeah. I just wanted you to know I'm going. If you can't take me, fine. I'll call a cab." She could afford it. With Fritz's money due to hit her account within the week, she'd be fine for a good long while.

Her energy level was off the charts. Prompted by nerves. Worry.

And that *thing* she had to talk to him about.

He was in jeans again, too. A lighter blue, faded pair. With a dark green pullover shirt. His light brown, slightly ruffled hair, the look in his eyes, just made the whole picture of him look far too good.

She needed breakfast.

And to confront what had happened the night before. Things were escalating so far out of control, she wasn't sure how to live in her own skin.

"I'll take you," he said. "And was thinking… I have a stop to make, too. I've already arranged for my brother to come here, but it might be good if you came with me. If you'd like to help with the case a little bit."

Wary, she wrapped her arms around her middle, needing coffee. Of course she wanted to help. Wanted to do anything she could do. But why was he acting as though nothing had happened in the hallway upstairs? Did he think they could just pretend it hadn't?

Could she do that? The idea wasn't horrid, allowing, as it did, the opportunity to avoid the difficult and awkward conversation she'd envisioned when she'd come down.

"Where are you going?"

"To see Randall Bowe's wife. I think I've found the connection between you and the other people who were recipients of his manipulation." He told her about his theory of Bowe supporting those who'd been victims of infidelity and punishing those who'd seemingly committed adultery. "He just got it wrong with you, that's all—since you were faithful and Fritz wasn't. His wife may be able to give us some insight as to his obsession. The police questioned her when he first went missing, but she was too upset to give them much of anything. Troy is hunting Bowe and I offered to follow up on this end."

"You want me to go with you to question the wife of the man who put me in prison?"

His gaze pointed, he didn't back off at all. "I want you to have the opportunity to be involved, if you want to be."

What type of man was Clarke? Seeming to be able to look inside her, see what she most needed, and then be willing to give it to her?

If she wasn't standing there living and breathing it, she wouldn't believe the past forty-eight hours had even happened. It had been easier to comprehend her butt in a prison cell than to wrap her mind around Clarke Colton.

"You know I want to be," she answered him quietly. "Thank you."

He nodded. Told her they'd leave at nine thirty, turned as though to head back to his office, and she said, "Gram's sick."

Swinging back immediately, he asked, "What's wrong with her?"

She shrugged. "Probably just a cold. I'll know more when I see her for myself. But…it scares me…her being there, her age, all those germs…"

"She needs for her attorney to approach the DA for a plea agreement," he said. And her ire rose again, instantly, as it had the last time they'd been on the topic. Astounding, the depths of emotion she experienced around him. Passion and its shadow side, frustration, like never before. "Or to consider the option if it's already been offered."

"She'd rather take her chance with a jury," she reiterated. In truth, Everleigh didn't know that waiting for a trial would be good for her grandmother. But the woman was of perfectly sound mind and had made her decision. "If the jury is made up of people from Grave Gulch, she probably has a good chance of getting off." The Free Granny crusade was ongoing, and growing, according to the news report she'd read the night before when she couldn't get to sleep.

He frowned, turned to go and turned back. "I don't want to piss you off, but...will you please just listen for a second with an open mind?"

She prided herself on her ability to see both sides of situations, nodded.

"Once members of the jury are sworn in, they no longer get to make choices based on what they think should happen or what they'd like to see happen. They become representatives of the court and are under legal obligation to make decisions based only on fact and law. And Michigan law MCLS 750.349 states that the offense of kidnapping happens if one knowingly and willfully seizes another with the intent to hold that person for ransom. She seized a toddler. And she sent a ransom demand. That's all the prosecutor has to prove, which they will within minutes, and the jury will have to make a determination based on that evidence.

"The mitigating factors will come in during the sentencing stage, so she likely wouldn't get the maximum sentence, which is life in prison. But she could get any other number of years based on other case sentencings of toddler abductions for ransom. And… there's an off chance that she could get off with time served and a fifty-thousand-dollar fine. Regardless, she'll be in prison for months, at the very least, preparing for trial."

She could cover the fine. So, there was hope. There *was* hope! Her trial had been considered speedy and she'd been in prison two months. Gram was sick. But there was hope.

And she stared at him. "You have Michigan law memorized?"

"No," he told her straight on. "I looked it up the first night you were here. And talked to a lawyer friend."

He had her back. Standing there with him, knowing that, she almost started to cry.

"But if, on the other hand, you leave this to DA Parks, she could be out of prison immediately, and maybe never have to go back. If that's stipulated in the plea agreement."

She stiffened. "How would that work?"

"If she pled guilty and the DA recommends house arrest while awaiting sentencing, she could be released almost immediately. The DA has discretion, and the ability to make recommendations to the judge, without a trial. It would mean that Hannah would have a felony charge against her, because she'd be admitting guilt.

But with the DA not presenting all of their evidence, but rather recommending that the crime only warrants certain punishment, the judge could be more lenient."

She shook her head. "You said she could potentially not have to go back to prison."

"The judge can sentence her to home confinement. And if that's what the DA agrees to, chances are good that's what she'd get."

Seriously. Not an option she'd had on her list. People from her walk of life didn't generally get the DA's ear. "You talked to your lawyer friend about this?"

"I did."

"And this is a real possibility?"

"From what I was told, it's more likely than not, considering the circumstances, that this could happen. Especially with the chief of police putting in a word on your grandmother's behalf and public opinion already being in her favor. And with the victim's mother willing to drop charges altogether..."

That option sounded so good. She wanted so badly for things to go the way he'd described. But getting Gram to plead guilty...to turn herself over to the DA and the judge without any of her peers hearing her side of things...

"Gram doesn't trust the GGPD as a whole," she told him. "She didn't even before my arrest, and then, with the subsequent mishandling of things..."

Everleigh had kind of thought the same of the department, too. But she'd had no real evidence to back up any allegations of wrongdoing until now. "You all seem to, I don't know, be unaware of how it feels to be on the other side of the law. Rightfully or wrongfully."

"Are you aware that my aunt, Amanda Colton, was murdered in a robbery home invasion right here in Grave Gulch? Troy and Desiree were toddlers and home when it happened."

She shook her head. "I didn't know that."

"I was ten at the time," he continued, "and remember it all clearly. My parents' horror, the way they watched over us kids so closely after. My dad constantly worrying about Mom. Our cousins stayed with us some, while Uncle Geoff dealt with his own grief. It shaped all of us, even the family members who came after. We all grew up with that murder as a central point in our family."

Shocked, hurting for him, trying to imagine a ten-year-old boy, the oldest child, dealing with all of that, she asked, "Did they catch who did it?"

The slow shake of his head was telling. "They did not. And that's why so many of us are in law enforcement—or some form of protection. A need for justice is ingrained in us all."

And that kind of explained why he stood so staunchly by the need of the court system to be just. For Everleigh, when the police had failed. And in Gram's case, too.

For her, it was new…having someone in her corner *just because.* Without asking for anything in return. He'd told her he didn't even want her money. Who did that?

"Would you talk to my grandmother?" she blurted before the idea was fully formed. Or vetted at all. "Since you're the one who proved my innocence, she'd like to meet you. And she'll trust you some, too, even though you're the police chief's brother. Maybe you could convince her that she can trust your family and that she'd be safer making a deal with the DA than going to trial."

He studied her for a long second, and she tingled under his gaze. "I have no problem giving it a try," he said. And she smiled.

Half an hour later Clarke was still feeling the dizzying effects of the full force of Everleigh's smile when he went out to the kitchen to find her making a lasagna for dinner. The woman was being hunted and she still made supper.

He liked the making-supper part…too much, and remembered why he was out there.

"Take a look at this photo," he said, showing her an image of Brenda Nolton that Ellie had just sent over. She'd already told him that the alibis of the other two women had checked out. "Do you recognize her?"

She nodded, frowning. "She used to hang out at the health club. I'd see her there sometimes when I went in to work out. She was one of Fritz's personal-training clients and fawned on him a lot. It was pretty obvious that she had a crush, but I never got any vibes from her that she'd act on it. It was more like a hero-worship kind of thing. Who is she?"

"Brenda Nolton."

"The woman with the record for fraud?"

"And last night someone confirmed that she and Fritz had been lovers."

She hardly blinked at the mention of her husband's philandering that time. Life was toughening her up. He wished it didn't have to do so. "Doesn't mean they were," she said, glancing at the picture again. "Someone could have assumed from the way she acted around him that they were."

He couldn't tell if she was wishful thinking or not. Didn't really seem like she was, but rather speaking her honest impression. But then, this was the woman who'd been married to a philanderer for years without knowing he was cheating on her. She'd seen what she'd expected to see.

He had to see what really was. And added another possible outing to their list of them for the day.

"Still, with Fritz's history, it's safe to assume he'd slept with her. At least once. If nothing else, I have one thing to be very thankful for through all of this."

"What's that?"

"My freedom. With all that's happened, seeing him for who he was… I'm completely over him."

Clarke put an immediate lid on the thrill that shot through him as he heard her words.

"You up for doing some spying of our own?"

"On this woman?"

He excelled at covert surveillance, so he felt fairly confident he could keep Everleigh safe if Brenda turned out to be, as he expected, her attacker. And if she did see them, she'd show her hand. Clarke had a better chance at protecting Everleigh on the offensive than if they were ambushed again.

"Yes."

"I'll do anything that will help figure this out," she told him. "But only after I see Gram."

He agreed, not altogether happy about the day's plan, but knowing that he couldn't keep Everleigh locked up in his condo forever.

Or even much longer.

She wasn't going to allow it.

Most particularly if he kissed her again. He'd like to assure himself that he absolutely would not, but standing there with her, he wasn't so sure about that.

Chapter 14

Everleigh went in to see Gram first and was relieved to see that she was pretty much just fine. A little bit of a runny nose. Something that she got on a pretty regular basis in the wintertime. She agreed to hear Clarke out, told both him and Everleigh that she'd think about what he'd said.

She'd responded to it in such a way, though, that Everleigh knew they'd hit home. Didn't mean Gram would agree to speak with DA Parks or to consider a deal. But she'd at least left the idea on the table to be further pondered.

Taking that as a win, Everleigh was feeling a bit more in control of things as she and Clarke arrived at the home of Randall Bowe and his wife, Muriel.

Troy was waiting out front for them and they all went in together.

Muriel hardly glanced over when Clarke introduced Everleigh and nodded in her direction rather than holding out her hand, almost as though dismissing her. Everleigh, not taking offense, was perfectly happy to just nod right back. The other woman, dressed in what looked like designer black pants and a long-sleeved soft and expensive-looking maroon shirt with a matching maroon, gold, tan and black jacket, appeared as though she was ready to head out to some highbrow lunch. In fact, she'd told them to come anytime. She wasn't leaving the house all day. Everleigh had heard the conversation on the car's phone system as they'd headed out to the prison.

And she stood there and listened as Muriel answered the detective's and then Clarke's questions. Other than seeming rather snooty, Randall Bowe's wife didn't seem like a bad woman. To the contrary, Everleigh felt sorry for her more than anything.

She hadn't asked them any farther into her home than behind the closed front door for warmth. She apologized for having been too upset to speak with the police on the day the allegations had broken. The only thing she'd said then was that her husband was away at a forensic-science convention. She hadn't even been sure where it was. Clarke had given Everleigh that much in the car.

She had a little more to say this time. First and foremost, the cities where the conventions were to take place—two, not one. "He said he was going to be in New York first and then Chicago," she told them, her arms crossed and her tone formal. Distant. As though, while she was cooperating, the questions were really beneath her.

As was their being there at all.

"I've done nothing wrong," she stated for the second time. And Everleigh wondered if Muriel's snootiness covered a bone-deep fear she didn't know how to handle.

It was something she could relate to. One hundred percent. To find out your husband was not at all who you thought him to be...

"We're not here to accuse you of anything," Troy said.

"We don't suspect you of anything, either," Clarke added. "But we need to find your husband, sooner rather than later."

"He hasn't been in touch with me at all," Muriel said stiffly. "He said he'd be busy, that he wouldn't be able to call every night, but he hasn't contacted me at all. In four days' time, with all this going on, he can't call me once?"

"Did he say how long he'd be gone?"

"Ten days."

And then, with a glance at Everleigh, she looked back at the two men. "He's not at a convention, is he?"

Troy pursed his lips as he shook his head. "We don't believe so, no. We haven't been able to find any listed, though now that we know the cities, we'll be able to confirm one way or the other."

She nodded. Hugged herself a little tighter. And Everleigh knew for sure she felt for her. Muriel was barely holding herself up—all alone in her big house in a town where her respected and successful husband had just become a pariah.

It wasn't a smiling time, but she tried to keep her expression soft as the other woman looked at her. Really looked at her. And then back at the two men.

"He really did it, didn't he?"

They nodded in unison. "Do you have any idea why?" Clarke asked.

She shook her head. "None," she said. "I've spent the past four days going over our lives together, looking for signs, things I missed..."

"If he didn't want you to find them, and you weren't looking because you trusted him, you wouldn't have been able to see them." Everleigh piped up whether she was supposed to speak or not. Some things just had to get out there.

Muriel's gaze turned back to Everleigh. "I'm sorry..."

"You didn't do anything." The other woman was going to have a hard-enough row to hoe. She didn't need to compound it with a guilt that didn't belong to her.

"We believe your husband was seeking revenge on those who were cheating on their spouses, and rewarding those who were loyal," Clarke said. "Do you have any idea why that would be?"

She shook her head immediately. Her eyes were wide, and there was seemingly no place her gaze could land where it could make sense of what she'd see. And then it landed on Everleigh again.

"I'm sorry about your grandmother," Muriel said. "I've met her a couple of times. She used to bake for the department Christmas charity event… To think that she's sitting in prison because of Randall… I just… I have to believe he didn't do it…"

"I absolutely did not kill my husband," Everleigh said. "Nor did I cheat on him."

"I did." Tears filled Muriel's eyes as they continued to focus on Everleigh, who didn't look away, in spite of her shock. She couldn't desert this woman who obviously had more to say and was struggling to get it out. "A year ago…I had an affair. Randall found out. I didn't want my marriage to end… I just… I don't know what I thought I was doing… Anyway, I ended the affair, promised I'd be faithful for the rest of my life, and Randall took me back."

"And were you faithful after that?" Clarke's tone wasn't unkind, but Everleigh was surprised how different it sounded than when he'd been questioning her. It lacked…a certain warmth…that she'd figured was a natural part of him.

"I was." Muriel's tone was emphatic on that one as, with a brief glance in his direction, she answered Clarke. And then looked at Everleigh again. "He brought up the affair a lot, though, to the point where it about drove me nuts, but I understood, too, and just kept telling him how sorry I was. I did everything I could to reassure him that it wouldn't happen again. I'd check in with him every time I left the house, though he didn't require that I do so. I just…"

She glanced at the two men. "In my heart…I know he did this." And then back at Everleigh. "I'm just so furious, you know? That after all we've been through, after all the groveling I've done, how hard I've tried…

he'd just leave without even so much as a phone call to let me know he's all right."

Everleigh nodded. "I know," she said softly, her heart in her voice. Because she did. Clear to her soul. How did you live with a man for so long and misjudge him? How did you hold your head up high after everyone knew what a fool you'd been?

At least Fritz had been only a cheater. Not a criminal who'd let killers run free. Who'd put question marks on cases handled by the GGPD. Suddenly she wasn't feeling as sorry for herself.

Or rather, as bad about herself. Her life might be a huge mess, but it was one she could clean up.

As soon as she was safe to get to it.

She wasn't responsible for ruining lives. Muriel had to live with the fact that her affair had most likely been the trigger that set off Bowe's crime spree.

"Your husband has a brother." Detective Colton spoke up. "Baldwin. Do you have any idea where he might be? Is he someone Randall might turn to for help?"

Muriel shook her head, seeming to be a mite stronger now that she had gotten her sins off her chest. Everleigh figured it would be a good long while, if ever, before the woman truly recovered. "As far as I know, Randall and Baldwin haven't spoken for years. And before you ask, I have no idea why. I never really knew Baldwin. And have no idea where he is..."

As they left, Clarke and Troy thanking Muriel for her time, Everleigh couldn't help but wonder if Muriel had any family or friends of her own. Any emotional support at all.

Getting in Clarke's car, she was a bit more thankful

for her own parents. They weren't perfect by a long shot. They'd let her down and she'd probably never trust them the same again. But she loved them, and they loved her still.

That meant a lot.

Conducting surveillance wasn't a hopping party, Clarke told himself. It took a lot of patience and mind control to be able to sit for sometimes hours at a time, staring at not much, waiting for something to see.

Sitting there with a woman who was so captivating proved particularly challenging. How did you control your mind, keep from thinking about something that was slowly taking over your senses? The sound of her breathing, her fresh scent, memories of the kiss they'd shared the night before.

That one kiss had been better than some of the sex he'd had.

They were parked outside Brenda Nolton's place—a little house on the corner of an intersection not far from downtown. He was a bit on edge out in the open. But so far had seen no evidence that they'd been followed at all that day. And if, as he was suspecting, Brenda turned out to be the culprit, he was on the offensive this time.

And keeping all four sides of them in view with the mirrors at his disposal. If anybody even so much as took a second glance at the car, he'd have Everleigh ducking.

"I didn't cheat on my husband." They'd been parked for fifteen minutes or so. She hadn't said much since they'd left Muriel Bowe.

"I know."

She'd been staring out the window at the house he'd pointed out as belonging to Brenda, but turned to look at him as she said, "But if I'd ever felt around anyone else like I felt last night when you kissed me, I might have."

Her gaze held concern. Doubt. Maybe even a hint of fear.

Everything going on… It had to be getting to her.

"You did great with Muriel," he said, figuring that was where her most recent train of thought had come from. And knowing that he needed to steer them away from what had happened outside her bedroom door. "I figured it might help, having you there, but it went better than I'd expected. She was on the defensive with us. But you made her feel understood. You got her to relate to you, to feel as though she wasn't alone…having a husband doing things behind your back of which you were unaware. The way you told her that it was a matter of having faith that made you see what you saw and miss what you didn't see, you need to remember that. It was so right." He wasn't usually so verbose, but the words kept coming. He had to keep talking.

To keep her from going in any deeper.

Suddenly, he didn't just have to protect her from a killer somewhere outside the car. He had to protect her from a "them" that was like a time bomb ready to explode right there inside the vehicle in which they sat.

He pointed out how Muriel Bowe had barely looked at him and Troy. About how her tone of voice had changed when she'd been talking to Everleigh. Commented on the exact moment that Everleigh had taken over the interview. Mentioned that he'd noticed even his cousin had taken a step back and let Everleigh run the show.

Everything he said was true. He was in overkill mode, though.

And when he stopped, she sat silently, not commenting at all on her very successful interview skills. He wanted to tell her that her level of compassion for others was unusual…and captivating. Shied completely away from that dangerous territory. Too personal.

Figured she should know that her gentleness was a silent strength, far more powerful than loudmouthed bossiness. Again, that was not professional and case-based conversation.

About thirty seconds after he fell silent, she sighed. And said, "Are you ready to talk about it yet?"

"Talk about what?"

"We need to talk about that kiss, Clarke. It's going to blow up on us if we don't."

Damn. She was the complete package. Couldn't he catch a break anyplace?

"Why do women always want to talk about things?" he grumbled. Feeling a bit desperate as he sought to keep them from sinking in the quicksand into which they'd already stepped.

"I can't speak for all women, nor do I think it's fair to generalize me into a group based on my gender."

He knew she was right, nor was he going to win this one. Failure was written all over it.

He glanced at her but didn't linger. Not just because he'd get turned on if he did, but because he had to keep his gaze all around them. He wasn't going to screw up the job, too.

Everleigh was not going to get hurt.

Not physically.

And that was all he'd been asked to do—keep her body safe.

"Do you want me to apologize?" he asked, with a bit of a tone, knowing he was being unfair. And yet… if he pissed her off…anger could defuse the situation. At least in the moment.

If nothing else, it might help them feel better to expel some of the tension that was building between them.

"Do you want me to?" She had an answer for everything now?

He glanced over at her again. And then turned his head away. "I don't know what you want me to say." He didn't have the answers. Clearly.

"I don't know, either. I just think we need to quit pretending it didn't happen. It's making my stomach hurt."

"The fact that it happened? Or ignoring that it did?"

"I don't know. Probably both."

"I find you incredibly attractive," he told her. Not wanting her in pain. "I've never known a woman like you. And I realize that us starting anything could only end in disaster. So, I'm choosing to try to keep my mind off sex and on the case."

"How's that working for you?" Her slightly sardonic tone didn't help.

"About as well as you'd expect," he shot back dryly.

"I don't know if this hurts or helps, but I'm not having an easy time of it, either. But I agree a thousand percent that to try to make something of it would be disastrous."

It hurt. A lot.

And somehow, her acknowledgment of their mutual struggle helped, too.

But before he could attempt to find a reply he wanted to let loose, the door to Brenda's house opened and out she walked.

Bundled up in a blue thigh-length winter parka with the hood up, lining her face with faux fur, she didn't seem to notice anything but the car in the driveway as she made a beeline to it and jumped inside. She started the engine, and he put his idling one in gear.

Showtime.

Chapter 15

Everleigh was distracted from thoughts of sex with Clarke as they trailed her husband's ex-lover from her home through the streets of Grave Gulch. Everleigh was aware of Clarke's hands on the wheel, of his upper arm muscles when he turned, but mostly her attention was glued to the blonde woman driving the car a few vehicles in front of them.

Clarke changed lanes more than Brenda did. He signaled and left the road, only to do a U-turn and return to the lane before he'd lost her. He turned once, sped up and rejoined traffic once, too. All, she quickly realized, to make certain that if Brenda was watching her rearview mirror, she wouldn't see them there right behind her. She wouldn't know she was being followed.

In those few minutes, Everleigh realized how very good Clarke was at what he did.

And was thankful all over again that he was not only on her side, but on her case. She never should have pushed him to talk about personal things. She'd known she was making him uncomfortable. She wasn't even sure why she'd done so, other than because her stomach really was in knots with the whole thing and she just wanted to confront it. Deal with it.

But the talk…whatever she'd hoped to get out of it…had fallen flat.

"She's going to the new gym," she said aloud as Brenda signaled a turn and then slid her vehicle quite adeptly into a parallel parking space out front of Grave Gulch's newest health spa. "I wonder if she switched before or after Fritz was killed," she mused. Interested, but not overly so. She felt no fear watching this woman. She just didn't think Brenda was the one who'd killed Fritz. Or tried to kill her. Just didn't get those vibes. The woman seemed too caught up in her own world to be attempting murder.

But Everleigh was a barmaid. Not a cop or an investigator of any kind. If Clarke thought following Brenda would help solve the case, she was willing to sit in that car for as many days as it took.

"Maybe she's got a new guy to fawn over," she added a couple of minutes later.

Clarke seemed more intent, now that Brenda was on the move. Watching everything around them, as though their suspect could suddenly spring out from behind a tree, instead of the door she'd entered through. Which was good. Kept them safe from touchy subjects.

Twenty minutes passed, and Everleigh was still

thinking about getting touchy. With Clarke. An idea was forming. It was stupid, inappropriate, completely unlike her…

And yet something within her pushed the thought forward in her mind. She'd been so good for so long and it had landed her with imminent divorce papers; a dead, cheating husband; in prison; and then with her grandmother in jail, with someone still trying to kill her.

"I don't want to die without knowing if sex can be as good as that kiss promised it would be." She knew all about promises, though.

In her world, they rarely came true.

Not if they were good ones.

And yet…even with all that had gone on…hope sizzled inside her. For Gram. For her future.

"You aren't going to die on my watch."

He'd relaxed back a bit, but was still watching outside the car the entire time. On watch, not just watching, she amended as her mind replayed his last statement. But he hadn't addressed her suggestion…

"I was thinking more about having sex *on* your watch. Later." She almost cringed as the words slipped quietly out. But she didn't take them back. Or even regret them.

His lack of response was not encouraging. And with his coat open, but covering his crotch, she couldn't tell if there was any other reaction from him.

She couldn't see his gun, either, but that didn't mean he didn't have one.

She knew for a fact that it was strapped around his waist, right where it always was when she was around.

Muriel had cheated on her husband. Fritz had cheated on her. And Clarke was suspiciously silent…

Did being faithful in a past relationship mean that she wasn't sexy anymore? To her former partner—or a future one?

"I'm free. It's a new feeling. I'm not in any way looking for a relationship. I'm coming off from eighteen years of sex with only one man, and while I thought it was good, as good as it got, I've got this very nagging suspicion all of a sudden that it wasn't all that great, as standards go."

"If you want to have a no-commitment, onetime thing sex with me, just say so." His words were a tad strangled sounding.

And she smiled to herself. He was strangling on his desire for her. She just knew that. And liked the sense of power that made her feel.

"I want to have sex with you tonight," she said. They were in a safe zone. Trapped in a car, unable to rip each other's clothes off. Or even kiss. "Just one and done."

He nodded. Never took his eyes off the world around them, but he shifted and she saw the way his crotch filled out. "Fine. Tonight. One and done."

Five words, spoken unemotionally, and her panties got wet.

Clarke knew he was a whole lot more versed in the sexual arena than Everleigh was. Worried that her innocence was part of what charmed him about her. Her fidelity.

He didn't want to be the one who made sex just

a physical occurrence, as opposed to the emotional commitment it seemed to have always been for her.

And figured she'd change her mind by the time they were back at his house, darkness had fallen and it was time for the deed.

The good man in him hoped she did. He couldn't speak for his carnal side. Mostly because he was trying not to listen to that.

Troy called to let him know that there were no forensic-science conferences going on in New York or Chicago, but police from both cities had been alerted to be on the lookout for Randall Bowe. His photo was going up in all precincts in both places. Troy and the GGPD were in the process of trying to track down Baldwin Bowe.

Brenda Nolton apparently worked out for an hour, based on the time she entered and exited the gym. She got her nails done. And she went for coffee with three other women. Gal pals, not mere work associates, judging by the hugs and laughs, and four-headed huddles. And then she went home. Three o'clock on a Saturday afternoon and she was already back at her place.

Didn't seem at all like a woman out to kill another.

Or to find something she wanted badly enough to kill for it.

"I really don't think she's the one," Everleigh said as they watched the younger woman let herself into her little house. They'd grabbed a sandwich from a drive-through while Brenda had been in the nail place, keeping Brenda's car in sight the whole time.

He'd heard back from his relative in Grand Rapids. Annabelle Belinski had an alibi for the entire past week. She'd been skiing in Colorado.

He was back to having no suspects.

"Let's head back to your place," he said. "I want to go through Fritz's things, one by one, read every ledger, if I have to. There's got to be something there that will tell us who he was close enough to, what he was into, that had him winding up dead."

"I'm fine to go back, but what if whoever it was really did find it last night? How will we know that it's done?"

Done. As in, she was ready to go home? To get out of having sex with him that night? Was she having regrets already?

"We'll know it's done when we find Fritz's killer," he told her. He'd stay out of her bedroom, out of her pants for the time being, but no way was he sending her back to that house alone. Not with a killer on the loose. "Whoever it is, they weren't just looking for something. They wanted you dead, too."

She shuddered. "I was hoping that they only wanted me dead so they could have me out of the way to find what they needed. Before I found it," she told him.

"Then why weren't they looking when you were in prison?" he asked. "Why did it start two days after you got released?" He'd been asking the questions for two long days. Was frustrated as hell that he hadn't come up with the answers yet. "The only thing that makes sense is that this is a crime of passion. Whoever killed Fritz had emotional ties to him. That's pretty obvious by the rage with which he was killed. And the choice of weapon. It wasn't a premeditated murder. And it wasn't self-defense, either, based on the crime scene. There was no sign of a scuffle. Nothing on Fritz that made it look like he'd been in any kind of struggle or had hit anyone. And no other blood at the scene except his. And afterward, whoever it was had to have hung around for a bit, perhaps exhibiting remorse. The way the paperweight was wiped clean..." He was watching Brenda's house, but knew that was a dead end, too.

Putting the car in gear, he headed down the street and turned toward Everleigh's neighborhood. He was missing something. And every minute that passed without him figuring out what it was was another minute her life was in danger.

"When we get close to your house, I need you to lie low." Clarke's words were the first spoken in close to five minutes. She'd been sitting there thinking about his thighs, his groin, his chest without a shirt on. Keeping her mind on the thing she wanted and off what she didn't want.

"With the car change, and you at my place, it's possible that whoever is after you hasn't been able to find you. They could be staking out your house."

Fear went through her. And exited, too. Fine. "Let them come at me," she said. "At this point, I'd rather ferret them out than be in hiding. No offense, I'm... um...kind of enjoying my little bit of time with you..." How could she not say that, when in just a few hours they were going to be naked? She really was starting to believe there might be something between them that was going to make her feel blissful. Just thinking about him naked was doing things to her that Fritz's body had never done. Naked or otherwise…

"But this is also like being in prison." She got around to finishing her statement. "A lot nicer prison, but still, imprisoned."

Although, being locked up with him in the room, doing things to her, was a possibility she was eager to explore. For one night only.

"I have to get home," she told him. "I have to figure out who I'm going to become. And how I'm going to get there. I'm thirty-eight, not twenty. I don't have time to waste." And she couldn't get it wrong, either. She'd wasted a good part of eighteen years, building something that had been nothing.

He was taking a long route. Crossing back and forth across main thoroughfares. She knew what he was doing. Making sure they weren't followed. And checking out the entire area before he actually took her to the one place the killer knew was associated with her.

Everything she owned was there. She had to go back sometime.

"Why not start a salon?" he asked, watching the area around them as he turned closer to her neighborhood. "You said you wanted to. You've already got the real estate. It's in a great location. And you said you're coming into some money…"

Way more than she'd need to remodel the gym. Some of the spa stuff she'd want—the tanning bed, the massage room—were already there. She was the one responsible for their presence, actually. They'd been her idea and she'd worked with the contractor to get it done.

The changing rooms were up front and could easily be renovated into stylist stations. The electric and plumbing were already there. The cement floor could be painted. She'd need padded floor mats for the stylists to stand on all day, to protect their legs and backs…

Her phone pinged: a text message. Probably her mother. She'd already called twice, and texted, too. Other than one call that morning, Everleigh had ignored the rest. She'd thought the party was lovely. She'd told her mother so. And that she loved her.

Her mother was seeking immediate forgiveness. She wanted things to be back the way they'd been. That wasn't going to happen. And Everleigh needed time to figure out the rest.

But, because it was her mother, and because Everleigh loved her, she glanced at her phone. And frowned.

"What?" Clarke's tone was urgent. Sharp.

With a glance in his direction, she said, "I don't recognize the number." And then felt the blood drain from her as she opened the message.

If you want to live, disappear now. Leave the state. Forever.

She tried to read it to him. Her throat was too dry, and she coughed instead.

He took the phone. Read the message. And, tires squealing, immediately wheeled around.

Back at his condo, Clarke had locked all the doors and windows. A series of officers patrolled the block as part of their nightly run. Everleigh hadn't argued at all when he'd nixed the visit to her place. She hadn't put up any fuss with any of the decisions he'd made since the threatening text had come through on her phone.

To the contrary, she'd been more subdued than he'd seen her yet.

Leaving him with a stringent need to make things better for her.

He'd called Melissa as soon as he'd seen the text. Ellie had confirmed what he'd already suspected; the number had come from a disposable burner phone, maybe even purchased right there in Grave Gulch. Officers were out questioning all establishments that sold burner phones in the past week, hoping that something would pop. They'd already vetted the third woman on his list of Fritz Emerson's lovers. She had admitted to having an affair with Fritz a few years before, had provided airtight alibis for the past week and the time of Fritz's murder, and was married with a baby on the way.

He had a client in dire danger and no suspects.

He also had planned a night of passion—which he couldn't keep—with a woman he had the hots for. And he couldn't leave his condominium…

The only way out was to find Fritz Emerson's killer before he did something he'd regret with the man's sweet widow. He made phone calls. Searched databases. Had Fritz's gym records sent over and started poring over them. Somewhere someone had missed something, and his job was to find it.

And then he had to get on to helping find Len

Davison and Randall Bowe. He had to help Grave Gulch PD and his family get their house back in order.

And maybe find a woman to hang with for a minute or two while he got over Everleigh Emerson.

She'd heated up lasagna for dinner. Brought a plate in to him. He didn't offer to come out and eat with her. Or invite her to stay.

Darkness had fallen, making it night. But he was not going anywhere near her. He'd never wanted a woman more in his life. Not even when he'd been a randy teenager and hadn't been with one yet. A fact proved out by how quickly his penis became erect when the knock came at his office door just before nine.

Damn!

He'd pegged her for going quietly upstairs if he didn't show himself.

"Come in." He wasn't standing up from the shield his desk offered his lower body.

"I don't want to interrupt while you're working, but I have something I need to discuss with you." Everleigh came into the room as invited, standing in front of his desk like some recalcitrant schoolkid. Still in the jeans and sweater she'd had on all day. Her curves were stunning.

"I'm going to my place tomorrow to go through Fritz's den like we intended to do today," she told him. "You're welcome to come if you'd like, but I'm going."

She wasn't. Not until he knew she could do so and stay alive at the same time.

"I'd go now, but it's dark out, and that would be plumb dumb."

He nodded. He could give her that one.

"Either I'll find something that will let us know who's doing this, or whoever it is will see that I wasn't intimidated by the warning and will show herself when she comes after me."

Right. That last part. *That* was why she wasn't going.

"It would be best if you were there, because of that second option, and better still if we had some police backup close by. But no matter what, I have to go. Sitting around waiting for something to happen… It's not good."

"It's better than being dead." He wasn't pulling any punches. Her life was at stake.

"The plan's solid," she said. "Use me as the decoy and we find the killer."

He met her gaze. Didn't like the quiet resolution he saw there. She should be afraid.

"You honestly think you're going to walk back into that house and take on someone who not only murdered your husband—if we're even right to assume it's the same person who killed Fritz—who's managed to ransack your home numerous times, almost ran you down, shot at you, and never left a trace for anyone to find? You think you're going to win that fight?"

"I just know I have to try. I'm not only our best shot. It's beginning to look like I'm our only one. This person's determined. He or she isn't going to stop and isn't following any rules that anyone in your business can figure out. It's like they're possessed."

Her calm tone got to him, the words she spoke even more so.

He hated them to his core. But she was right.

"If we do this, and that's a big *if*, then we do it my way," he told her.

She nodded. Eyes open wide, staring straight at him. She had no artifice. Nothing to hide. Another thing he loved about her.

Loved. Whoa. No. Just an expression.

One he wouldn't use again. Not in his private thoughts. Not in his dreams.

Never. Ever. Ever again.

He'd known Everleigh only a couple of days. Of course he didn't love her. He needed to get his head together. Quit making an issue out of an expression.

"I'll get organized with my sister, make sure we have backup. You'll need a bulletproof vest and a wire. I choose the time of day. The entrance. And you agree to follow every command I make while we're engaged in this endeavor." He sounded like an ass. On purpose.

"Fine." She turned to go.

He was home free for the night. Free to worry about taking her home to a possible death trap the next day.

And then she swung back, agitating his penis all over again. "Thank you," she said. She didn't smile, but he saw the softening in her gaze. In her features.

He nodded.

She left.

He'd made it through most of the night already.

Keeping her alive the next day would be a cakewalk compared to the hours he'd just spent, holed up in his office, afraid to trust himself to act like the decent man he was trying so hard to be.

Chapter 16

She didn't have anything to wear but jeans, sweaters and flannel pajamas in her suitcase. Would you dress sexy for a one-night stand? She supposed the question, while typical of her, was kind of dumb. Depended on the person. And the night.

Her panties were silk and low cut because she liked how they fit and felt. Her bras…more like something a grandmother would wear. She needed the support, too.

The bra came off. Sweater back on, the synthetic wool a little raspy against her nipples. Exciting her a little bit. The jeans…they were stretchy, but tight and wouldn't just slide off. No getting stuck in them that night. Having to pull them off by the ankle.

They had to go.

Which left her standing there in silk panties and a thick sweater.

Looking like a dork…with some pretty nice legs.

She tried the flannel pajama pants. Didn't go with the sweater. Took it off. Topless didn't work, either. Too bare.

Unless… Taking off the pajama pants, she stood there in her panties. Liking what she saw. Touched her breasts for a second, loving how they tingled at the thought of Clarke's hands on them. And, turning off all but the soft lamp on the bedside table, slid under the covers. That was the answer.

Wait for him, almost naked, under the covers.

Fritz had always said men liked unwrapping their women in theory but didn't want a bunch of fixtures and cloth slowing them down.

He'd liked her in nightgowns and panties.

In eighteen years of marriage, Everleigh had never slid beneath the covers wearing only a pair of underwear. It felt…naughty.

Sexy.

And fun.

Right until she dozed off and suddenly came to, realizing an hour had passed. A glance at the clock told her it was almost midnight. She'd figured Clarke would be working late.

But…what if he'd looked in on her and thought she'd changed her mind? Heart pounding, and not in a sexy way, she sat upright. Surely, he hadn't thought she was rejecting him? Had he changed his mind?

She couldn't lose this night.

The darkness seemed ominous, even with the muted light on. Hours stretched empty before her. The next day loomed, bringing possible harm to her.

Someone was serious about wanting her dead.

Someone who'd already succeeded in killing without getting caught.

She needed her fantasies to become reality. Being in Clarke Colton's arms, having him moving inside her… After tonight, those memories would be her happy place. The moments that would carry her through.

And if she didn't make it past tomorrow, she'd at least have known ecstasy once in her life. She wouldn't have died without living fully.

She couldn't believe she hadn't heard him open the door. She'd always been a light sleeper. More so since she'd been in prison. Just hearing Clarke come up the stairs had awoken her the other two nights she'd been in his home.

Maybe he was still downstairs working.

Or…maybe he was waiting for her to come to him?

The thought, once it occurred, brought relief. And a sense of rightness, too. Clarke wasn't like Fritz. He wasn't a man who thought only of himself. To the contrary, he made his living by thinking of others nonstop. Getting to know them, good or bad, figuring them out, so he could succeed in whatever mission he'd been given.

And his current mission was keeping her safe. Gentleman that he was, he wouldn't have come to her door, seeking what she'd offered.

He wouldn't push.

He'd let her do the seeking.

And the finding.

Or…change her mind without another word said.

Sitting up, she threw off the covers. Pulled on just

the shirt of her pajamas to ward off the chill, but leaving it unbuttoned.

She opened her door quietly, snuck out into the hall. And down a couple of stairs, checking to see if the light was still on under the door of Clarke's office. And when she saw that it wasn't, she made her way quietly back up the stairs and down the hall toward his door.

It was shut, but not latched. As though he'd left it for her to push in if she so chose.

Everleigh wasn't completely sure who she was as she pushed on that door. She didn't hesitate. Didn't feel the least bit shy. She might not recognize herself, but she knew for certain what she wanted.

She couldn't hesitate. She was standing on the brink of what could be her only chance to know what it felt like to be fully alive.

She knew, a second after she pushed open the door, that he was still awake. It was like she could hear him stiffening. Her gaze sought his as she approached the bed. This was a onetime thing, but she realized the night probably wouldn't end without more than just their bodies connecting.

She hadn't been aware of that, but when it came to her, it seemed as though she'd known all along. Clarke Colton was a once-in-a-lifetime man. She didn't just want his body. While she was with him, she wanted all of him.

And he was looking straight at her.

His worst nightmare and his greatest fantasy were coming at him all at once. Those long legs in his bedroom, walking toward him. The flannel shirt, unbuttoned, teasing him with glimpses of the luscious, unbound breasts…

He tried to swallow. Managed a gulp. Had to tell her to turn around and run. Couldn't get enough air and moisture in his throat to make words come out.

Or didn't have the brain waves to make it happen.

Either way, he lay there silently watching her approach, his body standing at attention, saluting her.

"It took me a while to figure out that you weren't coming to me," she said softly, wearing a smile that kicked him where it hurt the most. "I appreciate the consideration and hope I didn't make you wait long…"

She was almost at the edge of the bed and he hadn't lunged at her yet. If he could keep himself stiffly in place, tell her to go…he'd be home free.

Even as he had the thought, he knew full well that he was already home, and nothing was free.

She reached for the edge of the covers, was going to pull them back. He was strangling himself and couldn't stop her. So…

He helped her. Holding up the covers while she slid those long legs beneath them. Next to his. Smooth skin to his rough.

And he knew he'd lost the battle.

Clarke's lips met hers before Everleigh even had her butt on the mattress. Pulling her down to him, he settled her body against his and proceeded to wipe every thought from her mind except him. What he was doing to her. The touch of his skin beneath her hands. What was coming.

His hunger fired hers, consuming them both, and

yet he was gentle. So, so gentle. Taking her on a slow path to ecstasy. She wasn't even thinking about the culmination. Every touch of his hands and fingers, his lips, every movement she made on him… They were all the goal. And all filled with more physical excitement, more sensation than she'd ever known.

His tongue laved her nipple and she flooded down below. He kissed her neck, just below her ear, sending tingling sensations all the way through her.

She'd been well taught by Fritz how to please a man, but had never known that she could be physically moved while doing so. Just the roughness of Clarke's chest hair against her palm made her shiver. His back…his tight butt…all of it drove her further and further into a state of need that had only one destination.

Further.

More.

When her hand found his hardness, moved there as she knew would bring him the most sensation, he moved with her, against her, making it as much about her as it was his own pleasure. She grinned. And gave him more.

They didn't speak. There was nothing to say. But when she started to feel a bit adrift, a soul alone within the body he was pleasuring, all she had to do was look at him, and that intent blue-eyed gaze of his would sear her soul, bringing her right back to him. With him.

Even when it came time for the condom, he kept her engaged, her fingers helping him as he teased between her legs.

He kissed her, hard, his tongue dueling with hers,

and as he groaned, she spread her legs, letting him in. The first time he slid his tip inside her, she glued her mouth to his, sucking in air and then holding it. He made it home with one long, slow thrust and then moved a bit. Just little adjustments. Settling in. And touched her most erogenous zones some more. Softly. Teasing her nipple, he pulled out some and then pushed back in. Kissed her.

Had her going crazy for need of him. This man didn't stop. Didn't let her stop. He was everywhere, titillating every part of her. She'd never known anything like it. He didn't move from part to part on a downward cycle and then pump and be done. He continued to pleasure all parts of her and took the rest slow.

Until one last, deep thrust when they both cried out. She pulsated around him as he pumped his seed and their hearts pounded into each other, breast to chest.

Her arms clasped tightly around Clarke, Everleigh rode the waves and then relaxed with him on the mattress, still joined, still holding each other. Breathing together. In shock.

Wanting more.

They'd said it would be one and done. And she'd meant it. Still needed it that way. But one didn't have to mean one coupling. It could mean one *night*.

That thought was the last on her mind as she drifted off to sleep. And was still there sometime later when they awoke and made love a second time. And then, later, a third.

They never spoke with words. Just with looks. With touch.

And for the one night they had, it was pure magic.

* * *

Clarke always awoke with the dawn. Didn't matter if he'd had eight hours or ten minutes of sleep, light seeping in through the blinds got him up. That Sunday morning was no different.

He stretched as consciousness came to him, even before opening his eyes. And he remembered.

Moved minimally, checking to see how far away the second body in the bed had moved during sleep, only to discover himself with plenty of room.

Eyes open, he glanced on both sides, confirming what his legs had already told him.

He was alone.

A mixture of disappointment and relief swept through him. Relief won out.

If not for the lingering floral scent in the sheets, he could almost convince himself that he was as unentangled as he'd been the last morning he'd woken up in that bed. Would really like to believe that he'd just had the sweetest, most incredible wet dream any man had ever experienced.

After throwing off the covers, stripping the sheets from the bed and, still naked, putting on a fresh pair, he traipsed into the shower and stood there for another few good long moments. Get rid of the evidence and wipe the night away.

The plan was a good one. Solid. And he couldn't stop thinking about how Everleigh was both a vixen and nurturer, her softness and strength, the way she'd coaxed more out of him than he'd ever given before.

They'd said one and done.

He was sticking to it.

He wasn't the settling-down sort, and Everleigh was the most loyal, settling-down woman in Grave Gulch.

Shuddering at the thought of the last time he'd thought he and a woman were on the same page—the way Aubrey had been hurt and then out of control—he turned off the shower. That nightmare was far too potent, too fresh, to make him think, even for a second, that he and Everleigh could have a second night together. Or even a third.

She wasn't a woman who just had fun. And he wasn't going to give his conscience another mark to worry about—take a chance on another woman reading him wrong and her getting badly hurt in the process. Hurting women wasn't cool.

Hurting Everleigh… He'd rather die saving her life than cause her any more pain.

Downstairs was completely quiet, uninhabited when he got there, and he did a quick about-face, running back up the stairs to see that her door was closed. And he could hear movement on the other side.

She was still there.

Breathing a quick sigh of relief, he hightailed it for his coffee before he had to share the kitchen with her, and then holed up in his office.

He had plans to make, and then people to get with, in order to keep her safe, in order to have a team ready to save her, in the event that their visit to her house that day did bring her killer out after her.

With the warning having been sent, the perp was going to be watching to see if Everleigh complied and left town. And be agitated to find out that she had not.

Everleigh Emerson was not going to die that day. He'd die first. He'd die for her.

They might not have sex again, but he would always care about her.

He had an email from Bryce, who'd looped in Troy and Melissa. He still hadn't located Tatiana Davison, the murderer's daughter. They had to find Len Davison, before his next kill. And hopefully before the townspeople got wind that there was a criminal in their midst. They'd already lost enough faith in their law-enforcement department.

Troy responded that they'd made no progress on finding Randall Bowe.

Hitting Reply, Clarke's fingers flew across the keyboard. With some help from Ellie the night before, he'd done a thorough workup on Davison's two victims, as Melissa had asked. And proceeded to give the team more than they probably needed in terms of life histories, to conclude with the only information they really needed. Other than their ages and being unfortunate enough to both walk their dogs in the same park, there didn't seem to be any connection between the two. Which made it more difficult to predict, and thus maybe be able to protect, Davison's next victim.

By the time he hit Send on that one, he could hear Everleigh in the kitchen. And soon smelled bacon, too, whetting his appetite.

This woman seemed to have a knack for that.

And it just might be the death of him.

Turned out Everleigh wasn't a one-and-done kind of woman. She'd wanted to be. Had honestly thought she could be. But when, just before dawn, she'd woken up next to Clarke Colton, and the flood of emotion had entangled her, she'd known she was in trouble.

All she'd wanted to do, the only thing that had sounded right to her, was to cuddle up next to him and go back to sleep.

So, she'd quietly left his bed and retreated to her own world as much as circumstances and being trapped in his condo would allow.

She'd showered. And started to research what it would take to open her own salon and spa. She didn't need a cosmetology license to own the business, which surprised her, but she wanted one.

She wanted to be a stylist, too. She didn't just want to run the salon. She wanted to have clients of her own. To make people feel good about themselves. To pamper them. She knew firsthand how easy it was for anyone to lose faith in their value. To allow themselves to be used, in the name of being a good spouse or family member, without asking for the time and space for the self-care they also needed.

She'd been cutting hair at the center, and for her mom and grandmother, for years. For some friends, too. She'd had no formal training, but she'd watched a lot of videos. And just liked to fool with hair. With different styles.

So, she looked at the nearest beauty school, found out she could be licensed in just ten months. And felt stronger. More in control of her life. Like she had a purpose.

And wanted to run downstairs and tell Clarke what she'd found out. Tell him she was going to get things started with the building she owned downtown. Ask him if he knew a good business attorney.

A lot needed to be done: get the place licensed; contract work, acquire permits and schedule inspections... but that could all be going on while she was in school. It wasn't unrealistic to think that within a year she could be open for business.

But she couldn't go running to Clarke Colton.

She couldn't need him, want him or count on him.

They'd made an agreement. She was still a woman who stuck by her word. She hoped to always be that woman.

And yet...she was a woman who didn't trust her own judgment where the people in her life were concerned. But life was still good. The future promising. Gram had listened to Clarke. There was a chance she'd think about the plea agreement. For the first time in her life, Everleigh had more money than she needed—or would the following Tuesday, when the life-insurance money entered her account. And she had a plan for her future that actually excited her.

A plan that included turning into the woman she'd always wanted to be.

She could do this.

And get along just fine without Clarke Colton.

Chapter 17

Everleigh brought him breakfast—a plate to his office—and wanted to know how soon they'd be leaving for her place. She didn't look him in the eye. Didn't look at him at all, really. He could have been naked, instead of wearing the jeans and brown sweater he'd pulled on after his shower.

No…of course she'd have noticed that.

He just wished he was naked, with her standing there.

Wished he could slowly pull down those jeans…pull that black sweater over her head…unfetter those gorgeous breasts…

Instead, he told her that patrol officers were checking out her house this morning—part of his plan—and would be letting him know as soon as it was deemed empty and safe for their arrival.

That call came in while she was on her way out the door.

He ate his breakfast on the fly.

Patrol officers would be making periodic drive-bys until he let them know they were in and out. They would also be on call in case he sent out the distress signal.

He had this one.

Right up until they were standing in Fritz Emerson's ransacked office, getting ready to take it apart in a systematic order, and he pictured Everleigh there as the man's wife. As the woman she'd been, in that home, her home, for so many years.

She'd come alive in his bed the night before, a curious mixture of naivete and experienced pleasure giver that ate at him every time he thought about it. She'd known exactly how to please a man. But hadn't seemed at all familiar with the pleasures she could receive in return. Hadn't seemed to expect them.

Had, more than once, been wide-eyed and shocked by them.

The travesty sickened him.

He wanted to kick in the man's desk, stomp on his things, throw anything that mattered to Fritz Emerson against the wall and break it.

Because, in Clarke's mind, the dead man had done exactly that to the love and sweetness his wife had brought to him. And had continued to bring to him faithfully for so many years.

Eighteen years of a woman's life… Emerson had taken them, used them and then tossed them in the garbage.

Instead of unleashing violence, Clarke had to carefully look through the man's things. To get into Emerson's life, his mind, in order to find out who'd wanted him dead. And then come after his wife.

The fact that the newest ransacking focused almost exclusively on Fritz's office, where the murder had taken place, didn't pass him by. The threat had come to Everleigh to leave the state and she could live... Whoever was after her didn't have a personal vendetta against her. It had something to do with Fritz.

"I still think we're looking for evidence of a lover," he said aloud, breaking the silence that had been their almost constant companion all morning.

They'd said one and done. It was done. Nothing to talk about.

And yet his hours in bed with Everleigh were all he could seem to think about other than work. Other conversation didn't crop up.

She'd told him that she'd follow all of his orders, was pretty much doing nothing until he directed. So, there she stood, in her own home, in the middle of a room with drawers and cupboards open and things strewn all about, waiting for him to tell her what to do and how to do it.

He knew how he'd do it. He'd trample everything that didn't matter to the search. But he was in her home. "Let's get things put back together first," he said. There was some sound reason for that. She'd more likely know then if something was missing. Except that she'd already said that she hadn't been in Fritz's den since he'd moved out, until the first time they'd cleaned it up.

But she went into action so quickly, he didn't have time to change his mind. Just as they'd done before, he straightened and stacked, and she put away.

"What if, instead of a lover, this all has something to do with the building?" he asked. Needing answers. Needing to get her safe so he could get out of there and leave her alone. "We now know that whoever is after him wants you gone, not necessarily dead, like we first thought. Unless you stay in town. Then you have to die."

"You aren't suggesting I leave the state, are you? My entire life is here. Everyone I know and love… I'm not leaving Gram. Never…" She glanced at him briefly, but long enough for him to see the hurt in her eyes.

And his gut tightened. Everleigh was too sensitive… too deep…for that.

"I wasn't suggesting that you leave town. Just that… as we're looking…maybe keep your eyes open for everything to do with the health spa. Just in case."

"If this had to do with the spa, wouldn't it have been broken into, as well?"

"Obviously, whoever is looking for something believes firmly that it's in this house…"

"Or was. Maybe they found it and now just need me gone to do whatever they want to do with it." While he'd been stacking books, she'd gone to the corner with the tackle boxes. They were still intact this time, unopened, just out of the cupboard where she'd so neatly placed them.

Her theory held some weight. More so than his health-spa one did. "What would you being out of town have to do with any of it?" he asked, thinking aloud, keeping his thoughts focused. Her life depended on him doing so. "You still own the building downtown. You still own this home and everything in it. With you out of state, everything would still be yours..."

On her knees in front of the floor cupboard she'd been refilling, she looked up at him, frowning. "You're right, of course. So, what...?"

It made no sense to him. Meaning the motivations of whoever he was after were not making sense? That he'd been right all along, and this was a crime of passion? "We have to face the fact that we're not going to find a clear motive," he told her. Everleigh was in as deeply as he was now, in terms of this particular investigation. That had been her choice, one that she had every right to make. "And I'm back to being certain it's a former lover," he said. "Or, more likely, one who was current at the time of Fritz's death. She's not acting rationally. She's acting on emotional impulse."

"Maybe that's what she's been in here doing—removing any evidence that she was involved with him, so there'll be no proof to link her to the murder."

Now, that made sense. He grinned.

She grinned back at him.

And he got hard.

Everleigh tried not to notice the bulge in Clarke's jeans as she went back to work, straightening the room. A woman who was done with him shouldn't have been looking at the crotch of his jeans to notice anything getting larger there.

As she worked, she was looking for evidence, too,

but figuring that if whatever the killer wanted had been in plain view, it would be gone now. Taking stock of all of her deceased husband's things…recognizing some, not others…wasn't easy.

The book she'd bought him on tying flies… It was still the most read one in the office.

And the photo of him on the elliptical… She'd had it professionally framed for him to hang in his small office at the spa, but he'd chosen to keep it at home, where he did most of his desk work. He hadn't liked keeping records at the health club. He'd wanted them at home with him…

"We need to go through the physical health-club records," she said. The room was basically put back together. Enough for them to move around and know what they'd searched and what they hadn't. "He was funny about not keeping confidential information at the club… If something was important to him…he'd have kept it here." She glanced at the framed photo again. "Maybe there'll be a picture of the woman…"

Not that a photo would necessarily tell them anything. But it could.

"We need to be looking for a journal, a calendar, anything that might make mention of a meeting, a place, something that will tie him to this woman," Clarke said, going to the drawers in the desk. He pulled them all out, looked behind and underneath every one of them.

"I never knew him to keep a journal," she said. "Fritz wasn't big on writing…or reading, either…" Should she be feeling guilty, being in Fritz's office with the man she'd just slept with?

Would the old her have felt guilty?

Did it matter?

What would Gram think?

Back at the bookshelf, she shook her head, started pulling out every single title, leafing through them, looking for a written dedication, a name, any notes. Finding that on most of them, the bindings weren't even cracked.

She was thirty-eight years old. What her grandmother thought of her choices, while noteworthy, wasn't a decision maker or breaker. Yeah, for all of her youth, Gram's teachings had shaped her, but she wasn't a kid anymore. Not by a long shot.

And at the moment, she wasn't even sure she agreed with the older woman about the case. Thinking a jury was going to exonerate her because of circumstances… or worse, thinking that Everleigh's freedom was worth spending the rest of her life in jail…

"I called the prison this morning to check on Gram," she said aloud. "She's not feeling better, but she's not any worse." Yet. She'd asked for special visitation privileges again that day, just needing to see for herself that her grandmother shouldn't be in the infirmary. Being sick in prison…a woman Gram's age…with all the communal facilities, eating, showering…the gatherings during free time…

"That's good to hear."

She glanced at Clarke, watched him flip Fritz's desk chair, knocking around the bottom of it, as though Fritz could have hidden something there.

She wouldn't put it past him. But she'd never have thought to look there. Clarke didn't find anything. Put the chair down and moved to other furniture in the room. He was professional. Thorough.

And…he'd done her a solid, talking to her grandmother. She had yet to tell him that, with or without him, she planned to visit the prison sometime that day. "I was just wondering… When you said that about the DA being able to recommend, say, Gram not having to do jail time, and just being on house arrest, and maybe paying a fine and that a judge could accept that… Is there anyone you could speak to, personally? Could we get some kind of verbal promise that that's how it would go?" She wanted a guarantee, in writing, not just a promise.

Promises didn't mean the same to everyone. To some they meant nothing.

She was learning.

And she knew enough to know that the DA couldn't guarantee anything. The justice system didn't work that way. For good reason.

Her trust level might be in the red, but she still had hope. And an ultimate faith that life in general held more good than bad.

The night before had shown her something amazing she hadn't even thought to hope for.

What other joys might life have to offer her that she didn't know about yet?

She had to use her intelligence, her experience, to make the best choices she could make, and then hope for the best…

Clarke was looking at her.

"What?"

"I was just…" He shook his head. "Nothing."

"What?" Was he offended she'd asked for a favor? Like...she'd slept with him in order to get a favor? Or thought, since she'd slept with him, she'd earned one?

"The expressions on your face... They're fascinating to watch."

Oh.

What in the hell did she do with that?

"In answer to your question, you know I know someone who could talk to DA Parks. I know several someones. I have reason to believe someone has already spoken to her, and the information I gave you, and your grandmother, was a result of that. But this is all just talk. She'd need her lawyer to approach the DA to make the deal."

Her lawyer—the same court-appointed newbie who'd tried to represent Everleigh. And until Tuesday, Everleigh wouldn't have the funds to hire a more experienced defense attorney.

"I think the deal is there waiting," Clarke said softly. "I think any attorney could get it for her. She just needs to ask for it."

He'd already talked to whomever he needed to talk to. He'd already done her the favor.

Before she'd slept with him.

Did he have to be so darn...everything? Kind. Protective. Honest. Sexy. Fabulous in bed. The man was going to steal her heart whether it was good for her or not.

But she wouldn't let him keep it.

Unlike Fritz, Clarke had been honest with her about what he did and didn't want.

He'd told her from the beginning of their acquaintance that he was a man who didn't want monogamous commitment.

One time down the relationship road with a man who wasn't interested in lifelong fidelity was enough for her.

Chapter 18

Clarke finished checking the bottoms of all the furniture. He'd seen them used to stash drugs, mostly, but hidden space was hidden space. Especially pieces like the small leather couch in Fritz's study—the kind with lining stapled across the bottom, hiding the under workings of wood and screws. He was careful about removing staples; he wasn't out to ruin what had become Everleigh's property, but he carefully checked the full underside of the couch.

And found nothing.

Until he righted the heavy piece of furniture, dislodging a cushion in the process, and an empty condom wrapper fell to the floor. His first instinct was to snap it up and out of sight before Everleigh noticed. Which was ridiculous. They were there with the express purpose of finding the identity of any of Fritz's unknown mistresses. Evidence that he'd had sex on a couch in a room she didn't frequent should be good news, from an investigative standpoint. If any of the man's lovers had been there…it made his theory stronger.

And Everleigh was standing close, helping him right the couch. She'd seen the wrapper fall just as he had.

When she bent to pick it up, he cried out a quick "Don't!" And then added, "We'll want it tested for fingerprints."

She nodded. Stepped around the wrapper to right the cushion.

"It could be from the day he was killed," Clarke continued because he couldn't just leave her alone with whatever thoughts might be torturing her. Maybe he couldn't make things better for her, but she didn't have to endure them all alone.

"Could be they had sex, something went wrong, and she grabbed the paperweight in a fit of passion…"

"It always sat right there on that table," she said, nodding toward the end table right next to him. Not two feet from the condom wrapper.

"You said the other day that, while Fritz had seen an attorney and talked to you about divorce, he hadn't actually filed yet. That he'd been complaining about the paperwork involved…"

"Yeah, and maybe one of his girlfriends wasn't happy about the fact that he wasn't getting the divorce he'd said he would."

They were looking at each other fully for the first time since they'd made love. Thinking together. More energized, he didn't look away. "So, what if she thought there were divorce papers here? What if she figured she could present them to a court, and without you here to argue otherwise, she could have you removed as his heir, because if the divorce had gone through, you would no longer get everything?"

"It makes sense, I guess." She was frowning, but more like she was deep in thought, rather than feeling doubtful. "If she didn't know a lot about the law. His will is the defining document and that hasn't been changed. I'm sure it would have been in the divorce, as part of the agreement, but it hadn't been yet. Nothing had changed. Other than him moving out."

"And still coming home every day to work," Clarke added. "We've seen his apartment..."

"It was more like a generic hotel room." She finished his thought.

"He was sleeping elsewhere, but he hadn't really left home." They were on to something. He knew it. Asked her for a small food storage bag and used the inside of it as a shield for his fingers as he grabbed the condom wrapper and zipped it up.

"Maybe he told her that the papers included new will instructions," she said.

"Or maybe she's looking for the will, to destroy it." He'd moved away from her. He'd had to. Something was happening between them again and he wasn't going to let them fall back into that place where they did things that could lead to a future between them.

He removed pictures from the wall, systematically, one at a time, looking at the backs of them for anything that might be attached there, tapped on the walls behind them, checking for hollow parts that could designate access to hidden storage, while Everleigh started going through every tablet of paper, every business card, everything on Fritz's desk and in his drawers.

Maybe the lover had found things that would have revealed her identity, maybe she'd removed them, but that didn't mean the perp hadn't missed something. She'd have no way of knowing what random note Fritz might have made of an upcoming get-together or hotel reservation. What business card he might have pocketed and then kept.

They worked silently again. But more in unison than before, rather than the adversaries they'd seemed to be since they'd come back in contact that morning. She'd given him no sign that she wanted more than they'd agreed was between them. She appeared solely focused on the work in front of her.

That peeved him some, too, which made absolutely no sense. He'd never, ever, ever cared if a woman moved on. Which was part of the reason he knew for certain that he wasn't meant to be in a permanent relationship. He was always just one step away from the next brief time of sharing that would come.

No strings attached. Because after that first rush, the weeks or months of the love-getting-to-know-you-and-how-great-is-this time, expectations and then failed expectations leading to disappointments would follow. And that was what he avoided at all costs now. It used to be that he avoided being tied down.

He'd spent too many years living with the disappointments of the family he was already attached to. He'd seemingly been the only one to inherit his mother's artistic gene—unable to stay within the lines, to follow all the rules, because he'd seen life as a creative adventure more than a rigid plan. He was who he was, and he wasn't siccing that on anyone who wasn't already bound to him by biology.

He'd searched all wall hangings, behind them, above and below them, between them…and nothing. It was getting to the point where he might have to accept that either the killer had found what she was looking for—unless it was the used condom wrapper—or it hadn't been there to begin with. Pushing aside a credenza that Everleigh had already been through twice, he was surprised to notice how easily the heavy piece slid. And noticed the wheels at the bottom, attached to the inner part of the piece, embedded so that, hidden behind the legs, they didn't show.

Heart pounding, he tapped the wall behind it, but saw the slight line in the paneling that told him he'd finally found something of interest. There might not be anything there but a broken piece of paneling, a bad fix job, concealed behind a piece of furniture, but…

"You know of any damage to this wall?" he asked from halfway behind the credenza.

"No." Everleigh left the last of the cupboards and came over, watching as he tapped along the wall. Middle first, then top. Nothing.

The line had been right in the middle, right on a stud.

So, nothing again?

Kneeling, he checked the wall toward the floor and…

"What was that?" Everleigh came closer, squeezing in behind the credenza enough to see what he'd touched. "It sounded different."

"It's hollow behind here." He was already running his fingers over the paneling, looking for something out of place, an indentation or raised piece, anything to push or grasp, when he leaned against the wall with his hand as he shifted weight to move down a bit. Clarke practically fell as a spring engaged and the piece of paneling he'd been leaning against sprang open.

"Oh, my God!" Leaning over his shoulder, Everleigh watched as he removed the piece of paneling, revealing a small safe nestled in between two-by-fours.

"That definitely was not there when we bought this house," she said.

"You didn't know it was here?" He was working. He had to confirm.

"Of course I didn't." He could feel her breath on the back of his neck, wanted to wrap his arms around her like a shield and run with her until she was far away from the room. The house. The life she'd been living with a man she hadn't really known at all.

Instead, he stood, moved the credenza out of the way so that both of them had plenty of room in front of the hole in the wall, and knelt back down to the safe. "It's a combination lock, not keyed," he said. "You got any ideas what numbers he'd have chosen?"

She listed his birthday. Hers. The lotto numbers he always played. Nothing, nothing and nothing. He asked her for passwords he might have used that had numbers in them. Tried house and gym addresses.

"Try our anniversary," Everleigh said, standing in front of the safe, but off to the left of him. She gave him the numbers. He scrolled, turned back and scrolled the opposite direction, and then forward again. Freezing when he heard the click.

"That's it," he said, surprised. Why his anniversary? Unless, on some level, the marriage had meant something to Fritz after all. Considering that Everleigh had been the guy's wife, it made sense that the union would matter. Even if he was a cheat. Clarke pulled on the black knob to open the safe. And pulled out a sheaf of papers. Standing, he moved to the desk with them, Everleigh right beside him, and they pored over them together. Copies of the wills Everleigh had mentioned. A deed to the building downtown. His birth certificate. And some life-insurance papers...

"Wait..." Her tone had changed, grown sharper than he'd ever heard it. His gaze flew to her face and he saw the color leaving hers. The way her cheeks sucked in with tension as she gasped. And words stumbled out of her. "This is the insurance he uses... This looks like...the policy, but...this sheet on top...the beneficiary page...it's not me..."

She sounded...lost. Completely confused.

And...frightened?

Reading over her shoulder, he saw the beneficiary name.

Larissa Mead? "Isn't that your friend from the bar?" he asked, all senses on alert as he realized that they'd found what they'd been looking for.

She couldn't believe it. She was reading the document that would make Larissa the beneficiary of Fritz's life insurance and couldn't believe it.

Larissa?

That woman had just offered to have Everleigh stay with her. What, so she could murder her in her sleep?

Larissa was her friend. One of the few people she'd still trusted…

God, what a fool she'd been. Fritz and Larissa?

And he'd had the gall to accuse *her* of flirting with customers at the bar?

Fritz and *Larissa*? Had the two of them laughed together at how easily she'd been duped?

And Clarke…what must he be thinking…

"It's not signed," he said from just beyond her shoulder. If she'd leaned back, she'd have been touching him, body to body.

For a second there, she almost did it. Just let herself fall back into him. For a second there, she didn't think she had the energy to fight anymore.

To take any more.

But…what? She glanced at the signature line. He was right; Fritz hadn't signed it. And when she looked more closely… "It's not even the right policy number," she said.

"He never signed it. He never sent it in. He had it locked in his safe. This is what she was looking for. You're due to get your money on Tuesday. Fritz must have told her about this. She'd either thought the papers were signed or she'd forged them. She needed you dead in case she didn't find the papers in time…"

Larissa? She'd stood with her just two nights before in her own mother's house. Spilling her heart out. Accepting her compassion. All those months she'd worked with her, thinking Larissa had her back. When she'd been screwing her husband behind it…

"Why would she warn me to leave town?" Everleigh asked, because she had to try to process, because something needed to be said.

But before Clarke answered her, she heard a click, felt Clarke stiffen sharply behind her as his hand jerked to the gun at his waist.

But it was too late.

Larissa had beat him to the punch.

"Reach for the gun and she's dead."

All in black, she was standing at the entrance to the den, a gun held steady in front of her, pointed straight at Everleigh's chest.

"Why do I want you to leave town?" her former friend said, her tone eerily calm as she took a menacing step into the room.

Clarke calculated distance and movement time to the second. The time it would take a bullet to reach from the door to Everleigh's body. The time it would take him to shove her out of the way and take the bullet himself.

Too close to call.

"I gave you a chance to live," she said. "After I saw you…all you had to do was leave. Start a new life. Never come back. It's not like you had anything left here. You made that clear. All you had to do was leave." Her voice rose and Clarke moved the few inches he thought he could get away with, putting him that much closer to getting himself in front of the bullet.

"But no, you couldn't even do that right, could you?" Larissa screeched. "You're pathetic, you know that?"

He gritted his teeth. Engaging with her, taking her on, might be what every fiber of his being was urging him to do, but it would make the situation worse. Her eyes glazed with inhuman hatred.

"I've got a key, you know," she hissed, taking another step forward, shortening the bullet's trajectory. He'd have to shove Everleigh, grab his gun and shoot, all within less than a second. Behind the desk, out of the sick woman's sight, he pressed his hand against the back of Everleigh's thigh. Reminding her she wasn't alone. That he was there.

Warning her to be ready for whatever he might do.

"I broke in a window to make it look good once, but I've been able to waltz in and out of here anytime I wanted..."

Good, keep her talking. Gave him time to get his fingers up to the butt of his gun. To get an elbow a little closer in front of Everleigh.

"Why?" Everleigh asked, as though she'd read his mind. He believed her bewilderment. Her pain.

Larissa seemed to as well, and to revel in it. "We were in love," she shouted, a wicked smile on her face.

"When did that happen?"

"Months ago. He came to see you one night, but you were in the back, helping clean up a keg mess, and we got to talking."

"So our friendship was nothing but a sham? You've been betraying me all along?"

"Not at first, but after I met Fritz... You know how he was...so captivating... You have to put him first..."

"You could have told me. If I'd known, any of it, I wouldn't have stood in your way."

"He wanted to keep our relationship hidden until the divorce was final, because of his parents, so they'd like me. I told him that was fine as long as he proved his love to me by making me the beneficiary of his life insurance. If you'd just left town, I'd have had time to find the papers, to turn them in, and have the money moved to my account…" She faltered for a second, a sign of weakness that gave Clarke hope, as though there was something human left inside her.

"I meant, why did you kill him if you loved him?" Everleigh said, her tone flat, as though the two women were having an emotional discussion over a cup of tea. Or she was knowingly giving Clarke time to keep her alive.

"Because he had sex with me right there on that couch." She waved the gun slightly toward the sofa, and Clarke used the second to position himself more than halfway in front of Everleigh. "And then…" Larissa moved, too, advancing, and stepping to the right so that the top half of Everleigh's body was within her range again. "Then he tried to dump me!" Her voice rose, in volume and decibel. "Said he was going to try to get back with you! His family wasn't happy about him leaving you. In spite of everything, they really liked you…"

"It wouldn't have happened, me getting back together with him." Everleigh's tone was quiet. Controlled. Even…soothing. As though she'd talked down maniacs pointing guns at her before. "He cheated on me. I was done."

"That's what you say now...but then...ha!" She advanced another step, spewing spittle. "It was ironic, really, poetic justice when you were arrested for the murder. And then...sweet, little you...you get out. When I saw you in the grocery-store parking lot, I was so pissed I'd have shot you then if I'd had a gun. If he hadn't been there to save your ass, I'd have killed you then and there. Instead, I met up with a friend and got me a gun. I've gone through this house, getting rid of anything that could possibly lead the police to me, and now, thanks to you two, I'll have my beneficiary papers, too."

"They aren't even signed."

"Fritz might not have signed them, but you really think a little thing like forgery is going to stop me now?"

"That form is as worthless as Fritz was." Everleigh's tone was surprisingly calm, compassionate even, as she delivered the news. "It has a bogus account number. He did you wrong, just like he did me and probably a dozen or more other women. But you don't need to make this worse," she said. "You really think you're going to kill me and the brother of the police chief and get away with it?" Everleigh asked. "Think about it, Larissa. You know it's not going to happen that way..."

Even then, Everleigh was taking the high road. Trying to reason with a woman who'd pretended to be a friend while Larissa had been robbing her of her entire life. "There's no proof you killed Fritz, maybe it was in self-defense, but if you do this...you're done..."

She was purposely trying to take control of her life and get them out alive, or just doing a damn fine job of winging it. Either way, Clarke was glad she was on his team. She was playing right into his need to take another step or two before Larissa's hand tightened on the trigger for the shot. He'd have to move at the first sign of tightening. Any later would be too late.

"Maybe it will, maybe it won't," Larissa hissed. "But I'm damn sure not going to be the only one losing everything here," she said. "I didn't kill him so *you* could get rich and live the good life..."

The muscle in her hand twitched and Clarke shoved Everleigh...just as a bullet flew from the chamber.

Chapter 19

Everleigh saw the gun jerk, heard the shot, felt a deep pain and fell sideways, stumbling, tripping over her own boots, righting herself, knowing she had to stay upright or die. She heard movement, knew Clarke was there, but before she could process anything else, there was an arm around her throat and a piece of cold round steel pressed to her temple.

She wasn't burning. Didn't feel like she'd been shot. But she'd heard that sometimes you didn't feel it. Sometimes the site where the bullet hit the body went numb. So, was this what it felt like to die?

She didn't feel dead, either. Not yet.

"Come any closer and she dies." Larissa spit in her eye as she said the words. Everleigh saw Clarke then, still slightly behind the desk, his gaze cold, calculating, and his gun pointed right at Larissa. Her former friend wasn't going to make it out of this situation. As soon as she shot Everleigh, he'd shoot her.

His gun went off, or Larissa's did again. Everleigh fell to the floor, heart pounding blood through her—and out of her?—at a ferocious pace. She still didn't feel any deep wounds. Any burning or searing pain. Her leg hurt where she'd fallen against something, but she could hardly think. Loud noise came then, close by, within inches, and she opened her eyes in time to see Clarke with one arm around Larissa's upper body, and the other holding her hands behind her back.

She saw his gun on the floor, inches from her head. And realized that her skull—and the rest of her body—was still completely intact. That was when she started to shake. To shiver.

And to lie there, afraid to get to her feet.

She hadn't been hit. He knew she hadn't been hit. He hadn't waited for Larissa's hand to clench; instead, Clarke had taken his shot at the wall just above her head and dived in while she ducked, using his gun to knock hers away and then dropping his own to get her in a grasp she would not escape from. Larissa's weapon had not gone off a second time. And yet, as Clarke secured his perp, he wasn't seeing Everleigh get up. He *needed* to see her get up.

Oh, God. What if she was hurt? If he'd failed to protect her…

He heard a scuffle and then the front door burst open, followed by a flurry of armed officers entering the room. He'd known they wouldn't be far away.

He wouldn't have had Everleigh there without them close by.

But the morning had almost been a disaster anyway. Of the worst kind. Way too close for comfort.

Grace was immediately on task as she surveyed the room, heading straight to Everleigh; and as a couple of uniforms relieved him of his hostage, Clarke saw Everleigh sit up.

He took a deep breath. Let it out slowly. Started to shake. Blinked back moisture.

And went outside to meet Troy to give his report.

Everleigh assured Grace Colton she was fine. She hadn't been shot after all. Wasn't bleeding. And the shock was already passing. She didn't want to go to the hospital, to have anyone poking around. No examinations.

She didn't want anyone to know she'd recently had sex. And if she needed counseling, she knew where to find it.

She didn't really know what she wanted, other than to see her grandmother. To let her know that the murder part of their ordeal was over.

To tell her that she'd been duped by her own friend.

And, mostly, to beg her to tell her attorney to go to the DA for a plea deal.

She wanted to go home…and realized how crazy the thought was, since she was standing in her own front yard, coat on, arms wrapped around herself, still shivering, while law-enforcement vehicles arrived and various personnel did what they had to do. Her house was once again a crime scene and being taped off.

CSI had arrived.

Clarke was talking to Troy.

His job—protecting her—was done.

One and done. That was what they'd said.

She hadn't realized how horribly, horribly empty being "done" felt. On every level.

Where did she go now?

Funny, such a short time ago, Larissa had offered her house as a safe place for Everleigh to stay. And she'd actually considered taking her friend up on the offer. Betrayal bit into an already opened wound. She'd trusted so blindly…

Grace or someone would take her to Clarke's to pick up her things. Or she could have them sent over. Except, no, she wanted them sooner than that.

But sent over where?

Her parents' would be the obvious answer. No way she was going there. She just couldn't. Not yet. Not then.

And Gram's house… The thought of that was suffocating, too…being there alone, knowing Gram was locked up in prison because of her…

So…she could get a hotel room. The idea seemed so frivolous, but she wouldn't be short on money after Tuesday. Not that she'd waste it. She'd never be that far away from the wrong side of the tracks.

Her heart rate quickened as Clarke walked toward her.

"You ready to go?" He asked the question like they'd planned to be somewhere together.

"I'm… I can't really leave until I can get my car out of the garage." At the moment, there were several police cruisers blocking it. "I already gave my statement to Grace," she added, in case he thought she needed a ride to the station. She was assuming he'd have more official business to conduct.

"I know. I'm done for now, too. I thought I'd take you back to my place." He gestured around them. "They're going to be busy here for a while, collecting any evidence they can find of Larissa in Fritz's office the day he was killed. Going over the couch. Getting evidence from today. Proving that she used a key to get in your home multiple times. All of the things she told us are only hearsay in court. The cops know what happened, but they still have to prove it, or she could walk."

She nodded, having assumed most of what he'd said. "I thought I'd stay in a hotel tonight."

He frowned. "I'd feel better once we know that Larissa is locked in a cell, that she doesn't get out on bail…"

"Will that be sometime today?" She had to go back to his place anyway, to get her stuff. And if he wanted to bring her back to retrieve her car…

"Should be. They'll be interviewing her soon. She'll be booked on formal charges, get a court-appointed attorney if she can't afford one…"

Yeah, she knew the drill. Everleigh had been denied bail. Would Larissa be?

"If she asks for her attorney before she talks, the process could take longer."

That had been Everleigh's mistake, she knew now. She'd been so sure that all she had to do was explain and she'd be let go. By the time she'd been done talking, it had been too late to get an attorney that night. She'd been charged and put in a cell.

"Don't get me wrong," he added, his gaze intent but warm. "You're out of danger. You're safe. I'm just being extra cautious and would like to know that she's locked up, having been denied bail, rather than say goodbye and hear that she got out and has you cornered someplace. The woman is a bit too deranged for me to relax just yet."

He was the one who lived in a world of crime. He knew it a lot better than she did.

He wanted her to stay at his place one more night?

She couldn't do that. *One and done.*

"I'll come with you now," she told him, figuring a few hours would give them the information they needed for her to be able to get on with her life. She didn't have her car. Couldn't ask him to take her to his place and then to a hotel and then back to her car. Wasn't happy about the idea of trusting a ride share at the moment, but she was pretty much feeling distrustful of everything.

"You've been through a lot of stress, Everleigh," he said. "More than most people could endure standing up. All I'm suggesting is that you take one more day in my safe home, a place where you have your things, your room with a door that locks, and let the GGPD do their jobs, both here and at the station with Larissa, before you tackle the world again."

She liked the sound of that so much.

Too much.

Worried about the new danger she'd be introducing to her life if she followed him to the long, black shadowed loaner car.

But she took a step in that direction anyway. And then another.

Truth was, she wanted to go with him.

"I told Melissa I was planning to keep you at my place for now, so she'll be calling if they need anything else from either of us in the course of the investigation."

Did he know she'd been battling with herself? Looking for legitimate justification to go with him? Something told her he did. Which somehow made him more of a threat…despite the fact he'd just saved both their lives.

She brushed the thought aside as she fell into step beside him.

She'd just had a gun to her head. Held by a woman she'd thought was a friend. She was estranged from her family. Her husband had been murdered in their home by his adulterous lover, all while he'd been divorcing her. Her grandmother was in prison. She'd been in prison. Had no job. Her home was a crime scene. And the man who'd sent her to prison was still on the loose.

A few more hours to hide from the world wasn't too much to ask.

Was it?

The immediate danger was gone, but Clarke had never been one to walk away from a job until the loose ends were tied up. It wasn't done until it was done.

"Do you have work to get back to?" Everleigh's

question came softly, about the time they'd turned off from her road. She'd been silent up to that point.

Nothing about the near-death experience she'd just had. Or any of the events that had transpired that morning. Where, in his family, it seemed to him that everyone talked things to death, analyzing situations, regurgitating them until every fact had been dissected. She just... took it all in and moved forward.

He'd never thought he'd find himself admitting it, but he preferred the Colton way.

She'd almost died. He'd almost lost her. They should talk about that.

"It's Sunday," he answered. "I'll spend time poring over whatever I can find on the internet that can help the GGPD with the two manhunts they're engaged in, but other than that, no." If she'd been anyone else, he'd have asked what she had in mind.

With Everleigh...everything was different.

"I'd like to visit with Gram. I'd asked for permission when I called this morning, with her still not feeling well, and if you need me to go back for my car, I'll either wait for the police to finish and move their vehicles out of the way, or I'll ask them to move. But I'm allowed eight visits per month and the deputy director is allowing me special circumstances to visit outside visiting hours and..."

If she'd wanted to go alone, wouldn't she have suggested she get her own car two minutes ago, when they'd still been at her house? Maybe?

He liked thinking that she wanted to be with him.

Just had to not think about the horror he'd just come

through, thinking he could see her shot. That beautiful body, hurt in any way…

She wasn't his to ponder over.

Her agitation, her need to see her grandmother, was something he could help fix.

"I'll take you," he said. And added, because he felt the truth strongly, "I wasn't kidding about keeping you under protection until Larissa is officially locked up and arraigned. You never know what a lawyer can argue, what a judge will do…"

"It's Sunday," she shot back at him. "Court isn't in session."

He didn't see the issue. Hadn't they already decided she'd be at his place at least one more night? In that room? With a door that locked?

He'd said those things to let her know, without opening any doors to conversation about what was done between them, that she'd merely be sleeping at his place. That he wasn't, in any way, insinuating, hoping or wanting that door to be unlocked that night.

One and done. Because otherwise he was going to disappoint her, and she was going to get hurt.

But…to her point…

"Michigan's code of criminal procedure allows for judges to conduct business on weekends through use of two-way interactive video technology. That includes criminal arraignments and setting bail."

She turned to look at him then, those hazel eyes clouded with so many emotions she wasn't sharing with him. "She could be arraigned today? Locked up until trial?"

She knew the ropes intimately.

"Yes."

Her entire being seemed to settle at that point. Relaxing against the seat of his rented town car as though, finally, something had gone her way.

Everleigh's mind wouldn't settle. While the tension in her body eased at the thought of Larissa locked up, Everleigh's imploded life continued to stare her in the face.

So many things…

Too much to process.

Rationally, she knew she was probably still in the throes of shock. That her mind was caring for her by wrapping itself in a shield of cotton. But one after another, facts sprang on her. Over and over. Just facts. No understanding. Nowhere to go with any of them.

"I just wanted to let Gram know this part's over," she said. "I want to tell her in person." She needed to see her, to see that her cold really wasn't getting worse, wasn't turning into pneumonia. And to beg her to please put in a request to speak with her attorney.

His phone rang, and he answered over the car's system. Melissa. Letting them know that Larissa would be arraigned later that afternoon. She'd been in a private residence uninvited, with a loaded and cocked gun. They had solid evidence to prove that much, and it was enough for the DA to request holding her without bail. If the judge agreed, they'd be home free on that one.

And when Melissa heard where they were headed, she said, "That's the other reason I was calling, to suggest that Everleigh would want to head to the prison. Hannah McPherson decided to accept a plea agreement. A judge will take the agreement by video conferencing from the prison this afternoon. In light of the fact that she's not feeling well, the DA is recommending that she be released from prison, on home arrest, at least until sentencing…"

Everleigh laughed out loud. "Hallelujah!" she cried because it just burst out of her. But she quickly sobered, forcing herself to tend to the logistics. "When is the hearing?"

"It could be going on now." Melissa's voice filled the car. "Or soon. With everything going on, I missed the DA's original call on the matter. With all of the protesters outside and the bad GGPD press, the DA thought I'd want to know ahead of time."

Gram free? There was so much Everleigh needed to do. Get transportation. Take Gram to a clinic. Get groceries for her and…

"Your parents have been notified that she could be released as early as tonight and are on standby," Melissa added.

Everleigh wasn't going to stand by.

She was going to be at the prison…in the hearing, if she could make that happen.

The killer caught *and* Gram sleeping at home? All in the same day?

And Clarke right there, supporting her through it? The man who'd just saved her from a deranged killer. His timing down to the second. She wasn't going to ever forget those moments when the gun went off, she'd toppled to her side and no one had been hit.

He was also the teacher of a sexual lesson she would

never forget. The man who'd shown her that life held the possibility of unbounding physical joy.

With everything good happening, she could even wonder if maybe, by some chance of good fortune, she and Clarke could remain friends.

See each other every now and then.

Grab a beer.

They could meet in public places. Talk. And have no danger of ending up in bed.

Yeah…life had all kinds of possibilities.

And it was up to her to find them.

Chapter 20

Melissa's call was like a floodgate opening where Everleigh seemed concerned. After his sister had disconnected, Everleigh had thanked him profusely, multiple times, for the chat he'd had with her grandmother.

She'd talked about groceries, about staying with her grandmother that night…

"It sounds like your father is planning to come get her," he butted in, not wanting to put a damper on her joy, but wanting her prepared. "She'll be under house arrest until sentencing. Most likely with a tether…an ankle bracelet."

She nodded, still fidgeting, as though she couldn't keep herself contained.

This woman is almost killed, and she maintains a seemingly perfect calm, he thought. *She gets good news about her grandparent and she can hardly sit still.*

Yet another thing he found fascinating about her. She was an enigma, to be sure. One he was never going to forget.

She'd talked to him earlier that morning about her research into opening her own salon. He hadn't said much, but still intended to see that, if she did open, every Colton in the city would visit her. At least once. He might not be in her life long-term, but he could still help her have a good one. Then, and into the future.

The thought felt good. Right.

"I can't believe Larissa was sleeping with Fritz," she said then, sobering. And he figured the shock from the morning was wearing off. Probably eased on its way by the rush of good news.

"I can't believe I didn't suspect anything..." Her tone dropped. *No. Oh no. No, no.* He didn't want her to lose her joy again so quickly...

"How about that bit there at the end?" he blurted awkwardly. "When Larissa said that he'd broken off with her, saying he wanted to try again with you?"

He'd been trying to show her that she'd been the better woman. She'd won.

But as he said the words, more occurred to him.

Everleigh sat wrapped in her winter coat, staring out the front windshield, her expression placid. And he needed to know—for no rational, good or discernible reason— "Would you have been willing to try again?"

Did she love that man still? Think of him all the time? Mourn him and wish he was still alive? If he hadn't been killed, would she still be with him?

Not one of the questions was case related. Or any of his business. And he sat there, on edge, driving, making a turn, as he awaited an answer to the only query he'd voiced.

"No." The answer was slow in coming, but non-negotiable. "I admit, I feel a bit…vindicated…that, in the end, he always seemed to want me, for the long haul. There was that part of him, that when he was truly feeling a lack of confidence, he'd come to me and I could always make him feel better. I think maybe that's what kept me believing that our relationship was real, even when all the signs were showing me it wasn't. Knowing that I wasn't completely wrong about that, that I meant something, that kind of helps as I process all of this…but no." She shook her head. "I have not one single doubt on that matter. It's exactly like I told Larissa at the house. I was done the second he accused me of cheating. I can accept a lot, overlook a lot, but I can't live with anyone I can't trust. Nor will I ever be okay in a relationship that contained the possibility of infidelity. Ever. That's just not me."

So, there you had it.

She didn't mourn the creep who'd been perennially unfaithful to her.

And she wouldn't even consider any kind of relationship with a man who wasn't programmed to settle down with one woman for the rest of his life.

She didn't make it in time for the hearing. But Everleigh was standing there when her grandmother walked out of the secured section of the prison and into the hallway. Her parents were on their way, but for the moment, it was just the prison officials—one guard—and her and Clarke.

It wasn't until Everleigh saw Hannah, in ill-fitting pants and a sweatshirt that had been given to her so she could leave right away, that she took a truly easy breath.

Finally believed that she was going to get her life back.

Rushing forward, she threw her arms around her grandmother, hugging her slim, athletic form tightly. And started to cry a little when she felt those surprisingly strong arms wrap around her middle for the first time in too many months.

Everleigh was strong. Because Gram was her rock.

Always had been.

"Come on now, girlie. It wasn't as bad as all that," Hannah said, grinning, her own eyes moist as she pulled back enough to look Everleigh in the eye. "It's going to take a helluva lot more than prison to put a dent in the fight of McPherson women, right?"

Gram had been repeating the phrase her entire life. And her whole life, Everleigh had believed her. She believed her still. Which was why both of them were still standing.

"You really feeling okay?"

Gram looked fine. A little red and dry around the nose, but she didn't sound clogged up or hoarse.

"I told you I was." She had. Everleigh had worried anyway.

"So, what exactly did the judge say?" Everleigh asked as they stood there in a space all their own for a second while the guard talked to Clarke. "Other than that, you're released to house arrest until sentencing?"

She still couldn't believe the news they'd been

greeted with at the door of the visitors' entrance minutes before. Clarke had prepared her, but to have Gram standing there—a free woman other than the somewhat unattractive device on her ankle—was just so unbelievable. Almost too good to be true.

A part of her wanted to skip waiting for her parents to arrive, to just hurry out the door to Clarke's car—anything to get Gram out of there before someone changed their mind. Panic set in. She had an irrational fear that she'd never felt before the night, two months before, when she'd been arrested for murder.

"I got the fine," Gram was saying. "Only twenty grand, not fifty, and I will pay it myself, girlie, or rather, pay you back..."

She didn't give a damn about the money. Not even if it meant giving up her dreams of a salon. But twenty thousand was pennies compared to what she was getting on Tuesday. And there was no way her grandmother was going to pay her back. She figured she'd save that conversation for a later date.

"And I agreed to three years' house arrest..."

Everleigh hissed in a breath. "Three years!" She'd been hoping for one at the most. Still...Gram at home, rather than in a cell...

"I'm an introvert! I get to sit home and watch my shows. Not much hardship in that!" Gram grinned. Shrugged. Everleigh hugged her again. And then burst out the news that Fritz's killer had been caught. That it was her friend Larissa.

Her grandmother, who'd been whooping at the news of the killer being caught, sobered. "That's on Larissa and Fritz, girlie," she said, leaning in to speak softly, but her tone was still fierce. "Don't you dare find fault in you for their lack of character."

Trust Gram to get right to the heart of the matter, pull it out into the open. "I chose them," she said, equally softly.

"No, baby, they chose you," Gram said, her gaze grave, wide, as she looked at Everleigh. "You loved them back, but they chose you."

The look in Gram's eye… There was a message there. One she was going to make Everleigh figure out for herself.

Thirty-eight years old and Gram was still treating her like she was ten.

"They recognized your innate value, your tender heart," Gram continued, glancing over at the door a time or two. Looking for her son? Or watching Clarke and the guard, checking their continued occupation, giving the two women privacy to talk? "And your heart sees the good in everyone."

So, what, did that make her a fool? An easy mark? Was that what Gram was saying?

Something to think about…but not then. The door opened, and when her parents entered, the small hallway filled with a cacophony of celebratory voices and conversations. After a thankful and heartfelt group hug with both of her parents, one that healed without the words that would come when Everleigh was ready, she gravitated back toward Clarke, knowing he was there only because of her, and as they all left, she walked out beside him.

She'd expected a quick dash to the parked cars, but as they exited the building, they were greeted with a tunnel formed by long lines of people on each side. Some bore Free Granny signs. Others just stood in the cold with gloves and red noses and clapped. Everyone cheered as Everleigh, Clarke and her family walked by.

Emotion rose within her and she had to choke back happy tears.

She'd gone from town pariah to celebrated citizen pretty much overnight, and she wasn't any more comfortable with the latter than she'd been with the former. But Gram was grinning, and seeing that smile made the moment nearly perfect.

Clarke walking the walk with her did the rest.

They wouldn't ever be a couple, but he'd become a part of them, a real friend, and she was glad.

Clarke knew he had to get out. Get away. Melissa had texted while they'd been in the prison hallway waiting for Amie and Andrew McPherson. Larissa had been arraigned and was being held without bail. While Clarke had planned to drive Everleigh back to his place to get her things, walking through that throng of people with her and her family changed things for him. Irrevocably. It was a family walk, like at a wedding, when two people who were joined in front of everyone who knew them…

He was in too deep. Hadn't meant to be. But there he was.

Which meant he had to get out.

He wasn't the guy who'd fit Everleigh's life.

As they got to the end of the cheering line and made their way across the parking lot to the cars, he pulled her back a step and said, "Larissa's being held without bail and I've…got somewhere I need to be…" It wasn't a lie. He needed to be somewhere that she wasn't. "Why don't you ride with your folks and I'll get your stuff dropped off at your place?"

He had to cut it off at the quick. Make the break clean. No waiting around for her to arrive at some point. No thinking about what he'd say. What she would. No hanging around his condo with her stuff upstairs. No more temptation.

Or giving in to it, either.

The startled, almost lost look on her face cut into him. He bore the pain stoically. It would pass. It always did. "Uh…sure," she said, glancing ahead at her parents, arm in arm, and Gram, head high, walking a step or two ahead of them.

She looked hurt. Exactly what he'd been trying to avoid.

"Good, then," he said, grabbing his keys out of his pocket, his breath steamy in the cold air. "Would you mind telling them goodbye for me?" He nodded toward her family.

"Sure," she said, a look of pure confusion coming over her face as she stopped walking.

He couldn't stop. Had to keep moving.

"I'm glad everything worked out, Everleigh. You deserve all good things. It was nice working for you. Good luck!" he said and turned his back on her.

It was nice working for you?

Just be done.

It was nice working for you? They'd had sex, for God's sake. Spent the entire night pleasuring one another. Intimately.

One and done.

The one had been the most incredible night of his life.

And whatever had been between them was done.

Everleigh sat in the back with Gram on the way across town. Her parents wanted her to stay with them. Gram wanted her. She wanted to go home.

But there was no place attached to that word for her. Except, crazily, her room on the second floor of Clarke's condo.

His room, that she'd stayed in for a few nights, not hers.

She was going with them to Gram's to see her settled, maybe have a bite to eat, and then her dad was going to take her back to her place. She'd had a text from the chief of police herself, telling her that her home was no longer a crime scene, and Larissa was being held without bail, which she already knew.

She was safe.

And ready to cry eighteen years of sadness all over the back of her father's car.

It was over. She was finally free.

Two days ago, she'd have thought her safety, and Gram home, would have been all she needed to have her joy back.

So why wasn't her heart smiling?

She was out of prison. Gram was home, too. She was safe. They were both free. Fritz was no longer in her life and without the ugliness of a divorce. She'd rather have him alive, wouldn't ever have wished him dead, but being apart from him forever was good.

Really, really good.

Another day and a half and she'd have enough money to make her dreams come true.

And yet she couldn't think of a dream that money could buy. The salon, yeah, that was going to happen. She'd already told her parents and grandmother about the plans, and they all wanted to be involved, to help her get the place ready. They'd be okay. She'd always known that. Family love was unconditional. It didn't mean there wasn't pain, though. Or need for forgiveness.

But the salon…it was a career goal.

Not a dream.

When she really thought about it…there really weren't any dreams lurking in her soul, yearning to get out. Which bothered her. A lot.

She'd had dreams once, hadn't she?

As a young girl. Other than the salon, which she now recognized as a career goal, she'd wanted to be a wife and mother.

She'd become a wife—and the dream had died. But it hadn't been replaced with any others.

Something she was still pondering as her parents dropped her and Gram off at her grandmother's place and then left to go get fresh produce and perishables for Gram's refrigerator. Something Gram would have insisted on doing herself had she been free to do so.

Glancing at the tether on her grandmother's ankle, Everleigh had to remind herself that that binding was a gift. It was allowing her grandmother to be home, not in a cell.

"This thing isn't all bad," Gram chirped, moving through her home with the speed of someone getting to presents under a Christmas tree. Clearly happy to reacquaint herself with everything the eye could see and the finger could touch. "I get to be treated like royalty, having my shopping done for me. And all of the other errands that are like irritating piddles in an otherwise beautiful day…"

And that was Gram. Accepting what was and moving on to find the joy.

All her life, Everleigh wanted to be like that.

So how had she lost her joy without knowing? It was like she couldn't trust herself at all. Not to choose friends—or lovers.

How could Clarke Colton have just walked away from her as he had?

The thought sprang up with so many others, confusing her. Refusing to be stilled. To leave her alone to accept what was and get on with moving forward.

To finding her joy?

"You're different." Gram found her still standing in the living room just off from the front door. She'd done nothing to help with the homecoming. Hadn't opened drapes, though she knew her grandmother always kept them that way until darkness fell. Hadn't adjusted the thermostat that had been turned down during her absence to save on the electric bill. The older woman stood there, half glaring at her.

Because she hadn't been her usual helpful self? She deserved a glare for that one.

"Of course I'm different, Gram," she said, in place of the apology that had been on the tip of her tongue. "I've been in prison, I'm a widow, my husband was cheating with my friend right under my nose, my grandmother was arrested for me…"

The litany went on. As though, if she kept listing all of the things that had exploded her world over the past few months, the pieces might somehow fall into place and let her move past them.

"No," Gram said, as she sat in her chair, picked up the remote and turned on the television set. Chose a streaming service. A show. And then muted it. "Sit," she said, looking at the sofa.

Everleigh sat.

"Now, I know you're a grown woman and you don't have to listen to a word I say anymore, but I'm going to tell you one thing and you're going to listen to it."

Everleigh almost smiled. But because it felt so great to have Gram back, she nodded, straight-faced, and waited, giving her full attention.

"You are not to blame for anything that happened here. Not any of it. You didn't choose for your husband to be a cheater. Or for one of your friends to be one of his lovers. You had absolutely nothing to do with his murder or your arrest and time in prison. And, believe it or not, missy, you didn't have anything to do with me being in prison. I knew what I was doing, what I was bringing on myself, when I took that child. You think I had any plan of getting away with it? Of course I didn't. I brought him home, right here, loved him while I had him, and waited."

Gram paused. Everleigh waited. Was she allowed to speak yet?

When it appeared she was, Everleigh said, "I chose

to marry him. To befriend her. I did choose. I chose to trust them both, too."

"Ah…trust… Now, that's a tough one."

"I can't trust me, Gram. I don't have any faith in my own ability to know who or what to trust."

"You trusted that Colton who's been keeping you safe."

"I trusted him to keep me safe. It's his job."

"It was that man's family's job to prove you weren't a murderer, too, and they didn't do it. But you trusted him anyway."

Yeah, yeah, she got it already. She'd already said so. She didn't know how to trust good people. She trusted the ones sure to run out on her. Fritz. Larissa was just…wrong all over the place. And Clarke…

Thinking of him walking away from her in that parking lot. *It was nice working for you.* Her throat clogged with tears again.

She'd never have believed that Clarke would leave such a mark on her heart. That he wasn't going to be a permanent fixture, yeah, she'd known that was possible. But to turn his back and walk off with his *nice working for you…*she hadn't seen that one coming at all.

"You weren't wrong to trust, Ev." So many names her grandmother had for her. *Girlie* was the fun, happy one. *Baby* when she needed compassion. *Missy* when she was in trouble. And *Ev* when life was at its most serious.

"They were wrong to betray your trust. It's not on you, baby. Not unless you let what Fritz did to you, what any of them did to you, keep you from trusting again. That's on you. And then they win. Don't let Fritz Emerson rob you of the best part of you…" When Gram's eyes filled with tears, Everleigh was shocked to her core. Those eyes got moist sometimes. They never had actual tears in them.

But those tears… They spoke straight to her heart.

"He means something to you."

Clarke. She couldn't pretend she didn't know. It would just piss Gram off. And they'd still end up talking about him.

"He doesn't need or want me." And, "He's a womanizer just like Fritz was."

"How do you know? You judging him by that loser?"

It wasn't nice to speak about the dead that way, but she kept the observation to herself. "He told me he wasn't interested in commitment."

Gram's gaze sharpened. "Did Fritz ever tell you he liked women? That he wouldn't be faithful to you?"

"Of course not." She'd never have married him if he had.

"Then I'd say this Colton guy is already one notch better. A guy who's going to be honest about the women he's with is going to be honest to the woman he's with."

She nodded. No argument forthcoming. She didn't doubt Clarke's honesty. It was his desire to not commit that was the problem for her. "It's a moot point, Gram. He doesn't want me." As much as her grandmother would find that one hard to believe…

"You hear me asking about what he wants?"

She frowned. And remembered what her grandmother had said earlier. She went for the people who wanted her. But…

"You're a strong, capable, beautiful giving soul, Everleigh." *Everleigh?* That was a new one. But no matter what big-gun names Gram pulled out, she wasn't going to be able to convince her that she and Clarke Colton wanted the same things in life. Maybe he'd want a second night with her. She could see him being talked into that, after the passion they'd just shared. But then still done.

"And you're just plain sweet," Gram added after a minute, studying her as she spoke. Gram could give her that eye all she wanted. Everleigh knew what she knew.

"You know how honey attracts bees?"

Of course she did, but…

She loved the people who wanted her. Gram's words. Or a version thereof. Bees loved honey. But if you got close to them, they'd sting you. Gram didn't care whether or not Clarke wanted her…

Shock burst through her. Everleigh sat up straight, staring at her grandmother. "I give my trust to the bees that use me for their own nourishment, rather than…"

She cared for those who needed her. Who wanted her. She'd never allowed herself to go out and find the one she loved, the one she needed, the one she wanted.

She'd been sunk the minute Fritz Emerson had walked into her life. But he was gone. She'd been given a new ship, a new chance.

"He doesn't want a partner," she said aloud.

"Maybe not. That's life sometimes, too. But if you don't reach for what you want, you'll never get it. And if you keep spending all of you on those who use you up, rather than letting your heart soar, you're never going to find the happiness you deserve."

And there it was, the sorrow in her grandmother's eyes. Because her baby girl wasn't happy, and Hannah McPherson knew it.

Everleigh stood up. "Gram, would you mind if I call a cab?" She couldn't wait for her parents. Couldn't deal with them at the moment. Their time would come. Because love was love, even when the people holding it failed. Her parents loved her. Fritz hadn't. He'd loved what she did for him. He'd loved that he could always count on her to be there when he needed her. But he hadn't loved *her.*

Maybe no man ever would.

What mattered was that she was going to let her heart soar. That was the only way to reach joy.

Or to find a dream again.

Fritz wasn't going to win.

Her heart was.

Chapter 21

Clarke Colton was not a crying man. Didn't happen. Wasn't going to. But he came closer than he was ever going to permit again as he quit procrastinating and turned down his street an hour after he'd left the prison. He'd taken the long way home. Via a town in the opposite direction and then the backroads. Eagerly taking on unplowed country stretches, sliding on the ice and pulling out of the slide like he'd done in the school parking lot when he'd been sixteen.

The first time, he'd been in his father's fancy car.

He'd made it home without anyone the wiser. And grinning from ear to ear.

Most of his life had been that way. Taking the road less followed.

Doing what felt right, not what he'd been told was right.

And now, apparently, he had to grow up. Forty years old and he had to do what didn't feel right, but what he knew was right. He had to go home, get Everleigh's bag, take it to her place and never see her again.

Or he could propose to her, bring her home, have the best few months of his life until the newness wore off, and real life set in, and he'd make a case a priority, miss her birthday dinner, forget to buy a Christmas gift or take out the trash, and things would slowly erode and she'd end up getting hurt.

They'd split. He'd go off and find some other woman. She'd run into them downtown and he'd have to live the rest of his life with the image of hurt in those honest and expressive hazel eyes.

He pulled into the drive of the condo garage. Pulled out the card he had to use to get through the electronic security. The one he normally carried on his windshield was in the garage with the rest of his vehicle while it was having a bullet hole removed from it.

Card in hand, he pulled up to the eye of the device, the bar rose and his phone rang. It was Melissa, telling him that everyone was getting together at police headquarters and asking him to join them.

There would be pizza.

And no parents.

Pulling into the garage, he squealed his tires on the smooth cement and pulled right back out again. Anything was better than getting Everleigh's suitcase out of his life forever. Even a Sunday afternoon gathering of his siblings and cousins.

They'd congregated in the largest conference room. A place where DAs and lawyers met. Where the chief of police sometimes had discussions with politicians. Even in their not-so-huge city.

And it wasn't all of the Coltons in the GGPD. Just the ones involved with the Emerson and Bowe cases. Bryce, the FBI agent; Jillian, a crime-scene investigator; Troy and his sister Desiree, the part-time sketch artist, as well as their half sisters Annalise, a K-9 trainer, and cousin Grace; Melissa, of course; and Travis, their younger brother. As the CEO of a plastics company, Travis had nothing whatsoever to do with the GGPD, but had probably seen all of their cars and stopped in anyway.

Everyone was talking at once, as they did, standing around eating pizza, one or two leaning against the long table. For the first time in a while, the mood was a little less somber. "Granny" had been freed. Hopefully that would quiet some of the town's complaints against the GGPD—at least for the moment. It wouldn't last. Clarke knew it and was certain the rest of his family did, too. They had a killer on the loose. And a rogue forensic scientist missing.

But they were Coltons. They hung together. And took the good when it came.

"Hey, everyone," Travis called out. "I have an announcement to make!" Younger than Clarke by six years, Travis was as tall and muscular as his older brother. The kid was a bit of a maverick, making his own path rather than following their father in his business or the rest of the family into the justice and protection fields. Which made Clarke a bit fonder of him than some of the others.

He loved them all, of course. But hanging with Travis was more fun. "I'm happy to announce that Colton Plastics has hired a new co-CEO..." Travis paused, looking around as though making sure he had everyone's attention. "Her name is Tatiana Davison and..."

"What?" Melissa stepped forward, pushing past her family to get face-to-face with their little brother.

"What the hell?" Clarke said at the same time, advancing with equal tenacity.

"Are you nuts?" someone called out. Bryce, Clarke thought. He couldn't be sure. Nor did he pay much attention to the rest of the voices chiming in behind him.

"You can't hire her, bro," Clarke said, while Melissa turned red in the face. There were protocols. Things she could and couldn't do. Like giving out information that had to do with an ongoing investigation.

"Too late. I already hired her," Travis said, his blue-eyed gaze seeming more annoyed than anything else. "She's highly qualified, too, and she's in Paris at the moment." Travis looked between him and Melissa in confusion, backing up a step, as though they were seriously crowding his space.

"Her father's a killer," Clarke said, his tone low, but deadly serious. "We've all been looking for her. She's going to be brought in for questioning..."

And could, for all anyone knew, be involved. With harboring a criminal, if nothing else.

"A... What are you talking about?" Travis wasn't annoyed now. Shocked, if anything. But he definitely wasn't happy. "He was cleared of that thing months ago."

"There's been another murder in the park," Clarke said while the room filled with stark silence behind him. "Same MO. And definitive evidence that proves Len Davison was the killer. Randall Bowe destroyed the evidence that would have put him away last time, but it's a solid this time. I'm sorry, Trav, but it's seriously not good."

"And we seriously need to keep this in this room for now," Melissa said. "We can't let the press get a hold of this if we can help it. We've got to get this guy before he kills again."

All gazes were glued to their chief, including Clarke's, and while she might still be his irritating little sister, he was proud of her.

And told her so an hour later, after everyone else had filed out to head wherever they were going to spend their Sunday evenings.

"I'm proud of you, too, Clarke," she said. "I look up to you far more than I think you know." She coughed before continuing. "How's Everleigh?" Maybe he'd known she would ask. Maybe that was why he'd hung around.

"Good, I guess. Your text came through about Larissa when we were still at the prison. She left with her parents."

She was picking up pizza leftovers. Throwing away the trash. Grabbed a paper towel, wetted it and came back to the table.

"When are you going to see her again?"

"I'm not."

She nodded. Kept wiping. He hated it when she did that. Refused to react to him. To give him the piece of her mind he knew she had waiting there to dish out.

And then she did. "You're scared," she said, moving farther down the table, which pissed him off, too.

"You're right," he told her, straightening his shoulders. "Scared of hurting her."

Melissa stopped wiping, stood up straight, in uniform. If she wasn't his little sister, he might have been intimidated at the look she gave him. "Why on earth would you think you'd hurt her?"

It wasn't at all what he'd expected to hear.

"I'm not the settling-down type."

"You're here, in the town where you grew up, with a successful career, a vital and present part of the family, here for any of us, no matter what… How much more settled can you get?"

She was his sister. But she'd asked. "I haven't done well recently with women."

"Aubrey's issues weren't your fault."

He knew that. But still felt responsible. "She's only one in a long line, as you well know. I've never wanted to commit to anyone."

"Because you hadn't met the right one yet."

"I doubt that… Why?"

"You're a special guy who needs a very special woman. One who can hold his heart in her hands without trying to tame it. With that kind of woman around, why would a guy ever want another?"

Her words struck him harder than a bullet from her gun would have done. His little sister knew him pretty well, it seemed.

He had an untamed heart. Not a fickle one. He did what he felt was right, not what he was told was right. And he needed a woman who could live with that. Who could be happy living with that. Who'd want to live with that.

His wandering from woman to woman had nothing to do with an inability to be faithful. He just hadn't met the person who filled his heart to the brim…until now, that was.

"She won't care if I forget to buy a Christmas present," he said aloud.

"Probably not. She doesn't seem the type to pay much attention to the small stuff."

"Or the big stuff, either," he said. But that wasn't right, either. She paid attention to all of it. But she dealt with it. And moved forward on the course she'd chosen. She didn't sweat the small stuff. And she remained true through the tough days.

Kind of like him.

"Everleigh seems to accept people for who they are," Melissa said softly. "Genuinely accept them. I'd say a guy lucky enough to get her attention, to have a chance to win her love, would be a damn fool if he didn't at least try…"

He heard the words, but Melissa was talking to his back.

He was a risk taker, and falling in love was the biggest risk he'd ever take.

He had to get home. He was going to deliver the suitcase to Everleigh, as he'd told her he'd do.

And somehow, he had to figure out how to find the one thing he'd never looked for before.

The way into a woman's heart.

Everleigh's bag wasn't at her house. She'd taken a cab home. Talked to the neighbor behind her who'd come over to ask about all of the police cars at her house earlier in the day and about her grandmother. Apparently, Gram's release from prison had been filmed by someone in the crowd and put up on social media, making quite the local stir.

The woman offered to get Forester for her, but Everleigh had heard the hesitancy in her voice. "You want to keep him?" she asked the older woman, who already had two other cats.

"He does play nice with my girls," she said. "And he sits in my chair with me at night."

The cat rarely came out from under the bed when Everleigh was around. He'd been Fritz's pet, really. And Fritz coming home to work every day—his apartment had been little more than a hotel room—made sense now that he'd left the cat. And maybe Everleigh's heart hadn't been engaged enough to the pet Fritz had brought home without even including her in the acquisition. She just hadn't known that. And maybe Fritz had never really intended to leave. He'd come home every day to work. And he'd left his cat.

So, Forester was out of her life. Her house was no longer a crime scene. She didn't want to stay there, though. Wasn't even sure she was going to keep much of the furniture. Other than her personal things, she was thinking she didn't want anything from her life with Fritz. Who wanted reminders of being half-alive?

She also still didn't want to head back over to her parents' side of town. She needed time to figure herself out, her next steps, before they started grilling her.

Or trying to take over.

A hotel was the best option.

But her bag wasn't there. How did she go to a hotel without her toiletries?

She could buy more…but… Clarke had said he'd have the bag delivered, and she wasn't rich until Tuesday. Buying more of what she already had was wasteful.

Besides…what if he brought the bag over himself? Since he hadn't gotten it over there while the police were still in residence, even if he didn't bring it himself, she really needed to be there to get it. Either that or have it left out on the front porch in the cold.

So, maybe she hoped he'd bring it. It had to be that way. She didn't want to go to him. Look like she was chasing after him. He'd said "one and done." And she wouldn't make him feel as Aubrey had. She'd rather keep him for a friend than lose him forever.

Darkness had fallen. She'd had no dinner. Didn't want to cook ever again in the kitchen where she'd been so unhappy as a wife.

Why hadn't she seen? Known she was settling?

What difference would it have made if she had, though?

Once the question was asked, she had to sit with it. In the living room. In the dark. With a glass of wine. She'd have left Fritz if she'd known he was cheating on her.

She needed what she had to give. The loyalty. The fidelity. And the ability to hang around through the rest of what life had to throw at you.

The knowledge sat well with her.

She liked that about herself.

She liked the wine, too. And poured herself a second glass.

* * *

He may or may not have found what he was looking for.

A way into a woman's heart.

He'd been on it for a couple of hours. Had a buddy who, while he'd been rolling with Clarke's wild ideas since the fourth grade, now probably wondered if Clarke had finally gone off his rocker.

Didn't much matter to Clarke one way or the other what his buddy thought.

What was done was done.

He wasn't sorry.

Not about what he'd done.

He was feeling a bit bad that he'd taken so long to get Everleigh's suitcase back to her place. Most particularly when he pulled his rental car into her drive and saw her own parked there, outside the garage. She'd been home long enough to move her car.

There were no lights on.

And at seven o'clock, there was no way she'd be in bed.

Heart racing double time, he had his gun out of its holster and was running for the front door. If something had happened… Larissa had told someone about the life insurance…

He pounded on the front door. Hard. Over and over. Looking between the lock and the window. Breaking the window would be quicker…

The latch clicked.

Easier than either breaking the window or kicking the door down. Still holding his weapon, he lowered it. Wondered if she was looking out through the peephole, seeing him standing there like some kind of possessed idiot.

If it was even her on the other side of the door…

For all he knew, she had a friend over. He had no idea who her friends were—besides Larissa. Or what she normally did on a Sunday night.

But had a pretty good idea that sitting in the dark wasn't it.

The door opened. "Clarke?"

She was still in the jeans and sweater she'd put on at his place that morning. Her hair was a bit more mussed. Hard to tell about the rest of her. She still hadn't turned on a light.

"I brought your bag back."

No way she had a man in there.

Did she? Oh, God. What if she did? He'd given her no reason not to turn to someone else. What an ass he was sometimes. Cutting off his own nose to spite his face? He couldn't have blown this…could he?

Maybe she'd liked what he'd shown her the night before. Had gone out and found herself another man. She had every right.

And then some.

The woman had been faithful her entire life, and life hadn't been faithful to her.

She was free.

"Thank you." She opened the door, stuck her hand out for the bag.

He didn't want to give it to her and then leave. "Can I come in?"

He'd done worse.

"Of course," she said, turning from the door to flip

on the light in the vestibule. And then bent to turn on a lamp as they entered the living room.

His gaze immediately homed in on the bottle of wine. The half-empty glass.

He hadn't figured her for a wine drinker. Or much of a drinker at all, in spite of the fact that she'd worked in a bar. "You got an extra glass?" he asked. The bottle was more than half-full. It would do.

She didn't answer that time, but she left the room and came back a few seconds later with a second glass. Poured wine into it. Held it up to him.

All good signs.

And reason to put down the suitcase. Take off his coat. Settle back into the couch as though he'd been hanging out there all his life.

"This is good," he said, sipping the wine. Needing a gulp.

"I get it at a winery up north," she said, settling on the other end of the couch, those long, luscious legs tucked underneath her. "Gram introduced me to it years ago."

She didn't question his presence. Or call him out on his rude departure at the prison. She just…accepted that he'd come.

If he hadn't already been head over heels in love with her, he'd have fallen right then. Maybe he fell a little more anyway.

Maybe he'd be falling further and further for the rest of his life.

He could live with that.

"I have something to show you," he said, standing up. He wasn't going to wait and let wine do his talking. He reached for his belt buckle, pulled the strap through the latch, unhooked the latch…

"Clarke…" She'd taken a sip of wine. Put the glass down. But hadn't stopped staring at his fly. Of course, he was growing rapidly, so there was plenty for her to see.

But his penis wasn't the star of this show.

He undid the button on the top of the pants. Found it fascinating, and way too fun, that she didn't tell him to stop.

He wasn't even sure she felt the same away about him yet and she was welcoming him into her home, letting him get inappropriate without even offering an explanation.

Or a promise.

But he needed a promise from her. There'd be no more one and done.

No sex, period, until he knew the score. Knew that she knew. That they both wanted the same thing—one another, forever.

With his belt out of the way and the button on the top of his jeans undone, he'd completed the easy part. The rest…was way more tender than he'd expected.

Which was stupid of him, really, knowing, as he had, what the plan had entailed.

Lifting his jeans out away from his skin, he lowered them down to the middle of his hip.

It hurt like hell, but he got it all done. He had a plan, and nothing was getting in his way. It was how he rolled. How he'd always rolled.

When he knew something was the right thing for him to do.

"What did you do…?" Everleigh stared at the raw skin he'd exposed, leaning forward to get a closer look.

He waited.

"What…?" She leaned in even closer. Then looked up at him.

"You named your hip after me?" She didn't sound appalled, though he did detect a note of concern in her tone.

"Look again," he told her.

She did.

And this time when she looked up there were tears in her eyes.

"A guy can promise you his fidelity every day until the day he dies, but a promise isn't going to be enough for you. At least for a while," he said. "Because your trust was given in the purest sense and was twisted and broken." He'd planned more, but as the tears rolled slowly down her face, he forgot most of it. "I figured the only way for you to know for sure that my fidelity was always yours was to have the fact that I'm yours permanently emblazoned on me."

She was sobbing, which might have bothered him more if she wasn't smiling, too, and kneeling down. Her lips were even with the very sore tattoo he'd just had inked onto his hip: low enough that it would never show unless he was nude. She kissed it gently. And then sat back, staring at it. As though, if she looked away, it would disappear. Clearly, she liked what she saw.

He liked it, too.

Everleigh's. To show that he was hers, now and forever.

His buddy had done a good job.

And the rest was up to him.

Gently covering his very sore hip with his underwear, but leaving the fly undone because it wasn't at all comfortable, he sat down, holding both of Everleigh's hands, as she sat beside him.

"I know we've only known each other a few days," he said. "And that you're a recent widow, though I think that's less of an issue…but… I'm forty years old, Everleigh, and I've realized I've spent my whole life waiting for you. I don't want to waste any more time.

"Unless, of course, you need it," he amended. "I'm probably not going to make it home in time for the dinner you spend two hours cooking, and I'll get on a case and forget to call, and sometimes I get an urge to see if I can catch a fish with my bare hands in an ocean full of sharks…but I can promise you that, while I don't always follow the rules of polite society, I always abide by the law, and I will always, always, always be faithful to you. I love you," he told her, as serious as he'd ever been.

"I love you, too," she said while crying again. Harder. And even that he figured out. She had a lifetime of grief to expel. And a lifetime of the promise of happiness surging through her, too.

"I'm sorry," she said, sniffling, wiping her eyes and smiling, too. "I never cry. But I do need to ask you something."

"Shoot." He'd tattooed himself for her. He'd happily committed his life to her. He could handle whatever else she needed.

"Clarke Colton, will you marry me?"

His lips trembled. His eyes grew moist. His darling, sweet and so-strong Everleigh was asking for what *she* wanted.

"As soon as it can be arranged," he told her. And then kissed her until neither one of them had any air left in their lungs.

He sucked in breath only when he had no other choice. He'd found a way into his woman's heart and never, ever wanted to leave.

"And…do you mind if we get out of here? Before we've had too much to drink to be able to drive? I've realized I hate this place, Clarke. I want to go home."

Home.

She meant his condo.

Their home. He could hardly comprehend all of the changes that were happening so rapidly. Could hardly comprehend the opportunity and open doors they were bringing into his life.

The condo had always just been a place to him.

But Everleigh had made it a home.

Her home. With him. And whoever else they brought into their family.

Maybe the child she'd once said she wanted. She was only thirty-eight. There'd be precautions, but he knew that there were things that could be done to see a child safely into the world into a woman's forties.

But for starters… "How do you feel about dogs?"

"I love them."

"I'm thinking two," he said. And maybe two kids, too. If they were lucky.

"Two's a good number," she agreed, smiling. Holding both of his hands. "For dogs…and other family members. If it works out that way."

"I have a feeling that, if you want it badly enough, it will work out that way," he told her, pulling her up and into his arms.

When she smiled, he kissed her hard. And long.

And then, grabbing their coats and the bag he'd left by the door, he took her home.

* * * * *

Don't miss Book One in the
Coltons of Grave Gulch series

Colton's Dangerous Liaison *by Regan Black*

And keep an eye out for Book Three

Colton's Nursery Hideout *by Dana Nussio*

Available in March 2021 from
Harlequin Romantic Suspense!

Journalist Neema Kamau will risk anything to uncover the truth. She'll even get close to politician Davis Black in order to investigate his possible organized crime connections. But when her professional interest turns personal, the stalker who's circling them both might rob her of the chance to make things right...

Read on for a sneak preview of
Stalked by Secrets,
the next thrilling romance in
Deborah Fletcher Mello's
To Serve and Seduce miniseries.

Neema suddenly sat upright, pulling a closed fist to her mouth. "I'm sorry. There's something we need to talk about first..." she started. "There's something important I need to tell you."

Davis straightened, dropping his palm to his crotch to hide his very visible erection. "I'm sorry. I was moving too fast. I didn't mean—"

"No, that's not—"

Titus suddenly barked near the front door, the fur around his neck standing on end. He growled, a low, deep, brusque snarl that vibrated loudly through the room. Davis stood abruptly and moved to peer out the front window. Titus barked again and Davis went to the front door, stopping first to grab his gun.

Neema paused the sound system, the room going quiet save Titus's barking. She backed her way into the corner, her eyes wide. She stood perfectly still, listening to see if she could hear what Titus heard as she watched Davis move from one window to another, looking out to the street.

"Go sit," Davis said to the dog, finally breaking through the quiet. "It's just a raccoon." He heaved a sigh of relief as he turned back to Neema. "Sorry about that. I'm a little on edge. Since that drive-by, every strange noise makes me nervous."

"Better safe than sorry," she muttered.

Davis moved to her side and kissed her, wrapping his arms tightly around her torso. "If I made you uncomfortable before, I apologize. I would never—"

"You didn't," Neema said, interrupting him. "It was fine. It was…good…and I was enjoying myself. I just… well…" She was suddenly stammering, trying to find the words to explain herself. Because she needed to come clean about everything before they took things any further. Davis needed to know the truth.